Transporter Room One
to Captain Picard

"Sir," said the operator, "a crewman just arrived on my transporter pad."

The captain glanced at Ben Zoma, who shrugged his shoulders. Obviously he didn't know any more about it than Picard did.

"I didn't order any transports," the captain noted. An even more disturbing question came to mind. "Exactly where did she beam here *from,* Mr. Refsland? There aren't any vessels registering on our sensors."

"That's not clear, sir," Refsland replied. "My instruments tell me she came from the direction of the anomaly. But that doesn't seem possible."

"And who is it?"

A pause. "I'm not certain," said Refsland.

"I hope this isn't a joke, Mr. Refsland, because I'm not in the mood."

"I recognize her," said the transporter operator. "I just don't know *which* Lieutenant Asmund it is."

As if on cue, both Idun and Gerda turned to look at the captain. Now he was *certain* that it was a joke.

"Mr. Refsland," he said slowly, *"both* Lieutenant Asmunds are here with me on the bridge."

STAR TREK®

STARGAZER
THREE

Michael Jan Friedman

Based upon *Star Trek:*
The Next Generation®
created by Gene Roddenberry

POCKET BOOKS
New York   London   Toronto   Sydney   Singapore

An *Original* Publication of POCKET BOOKS

POCKET BOOKS, a division of Simon & Schuster, Inc.
1230 Avenue of the Americas, New York, NY 10020

This book is published by Pocket Books, a division of
Simon & Schuster, Inc., under exclusive license from
Paramount Pictures.

ISBN: 0-7434-4852-9

First Pocket Books printing August 2003

10 9 8 7 6 5 4 3 2 1

POCKET and colophon are registered trademarks of
Simon & Schuster, Inc.

Printed in the U.S.A.

For information regarding special discounts for bulk purchases,
please contact Simon & Schuster Special Sales at 1-800-456-6798
or business@simonandschuster.com

In Memoriam

My friend Adam died two years ago on September 11, 2001, a victim of the attack on the World Trade Center. He worked for Cantor Fitzgerald on what was the 101st floor of Tower One.

Adam was a bull, a physically powerful man who could easily have bench-pressed me if he had wished. His strength was evident in his racquetball game, which few people knew as well as I did, since I had played him on and off for nearly twenty years. His serves were rockets, his volleys laser shots. And it was his style to go full tilt after every ball in play, no matter how remote his chances of hitting it, no matter what kind of toll it took on his body.

If he lost a point, it would get him mad. And if I told him it was a good effort, it would only get him madder. "It wasn't a good effort," he would tell me. "It sucked. Now shut up and serve." It was his way of firing himself up, rallying his resources.

Adam lived his whole life that way—full tilt, take no prisoners. As his wife, Fern, would tell you, he wasn't reserved by nature and he didn't believe in moderation.

Some years ago, we were about to start a paintball game in the wilds of Pennsylvania when he saw that a player on the opposing side was wearing a Nazi armband for a lark. Adam, being a Jew, demanded that the player take the armband off. In fact, he was willing to take on not only the player but the player's half-dozen friends in order to make his point.

He made it. The guy took the armband off.

Adam was also a *Star Trek* fan, and a big one. We would often stand in the parking lot after a racquetball game and talk about the latest TV episode or Pocket novel. And the remarkable thing was how reverent he sounded in those discussions, how admiring of the people who came up with the stories he enjoyed. He was like a little kid, dreaming little-kid dreams.

So when I got the chance to dramatize Jean-Luc Picard's battlefield commission in *The Valiant,* I gave Picard's predecessor Adam's last name and I made his first name an amalgam of Adam's kids' names. If I told you he got a kick out of it, it would be an understatement. He held *The Valiant* in his hands as if it were the holiest relic he could imagine, the highest honor. And though I knew he would be happy about what I'd done, I underestimated his gratitude.

After all, he had become a part of the *Star Trek* mythos.

In retrospect, I'm unutterably glad that I was able to do that for him. Had I waited even a year, he would never have known about it.

I don't know exactly how Adam perished. More than likely, because of where he was in the building, he never knew what hit him. But I like to think he died trying to help others to escape, because that's unquestionably what he would have done if he had survived long enough. He would have picked up one of the injured in those big arms of his and ignored his own safety to get that person out.

And I can tell you it wouldn't have been just a "good effort." It would have been a *great* one.

Acknowledgments

This time around, the author would like to thank Margaret Clark, editor extraordinaire, for her loyalty, dedication, and meticulous attention to detail; Scott Shannon, the best darn publisher a guy could have; and Paula Block of Viacom, whose insight and understanding have been invaluable in this and so many other projects.

Also deserving of praise are science guru Dave Domelen, the always-witty Bob Manojlovich, Jim McCain (whose crab boil may actually get used some day), Mel Orr, Ryan McReynolds and his brother Scott, Simon Cooper, Geoff Trowbridge, the mysterious Derek, Todd Kogutt, and Michael Schuster, for reasons many and varied.

Finally, the author would like to acknowledge his lovely wife and two remarkable sons, whose forbearance allowed him to complete this tome more or less on time.

Chapter One

GERDA ASMUND had developed a certain level of awareness as a child, a sensitivity that came close to the level of pure, untutored instinct.

At the moment, as she studied the updated data on her navigation monitor to see what kind of hazards awaited the *Stargazer* in the solar system they were approaching, that awareness told her she was being watched. But it was experience that told her by whom.

Turning to her twin sister, Idun, who was sitting at the helm panel beside her, she said in a soft voice, "Just behind you and to the right. At the engineering console."

Idun's brow creased ever so slightly. Then she cast a glance over her shoulder in the indicated direction. When she returned her attention to her helm controls, it was with an air of puzzlement so subtle and unobtrusive that only her sister was likely to recognize it.

"Refsland?" said Idun.

William Refsland was the ship's senior transporter operator—an efficient and responsible member of the crew, by all accounts. But he displayed what was, in Gerda's estimate, a single very annoying habit.

"He keeps staring at us," she told her sister.

Idun smiled.

"What's so funny?" Gerda asked.

"I'll bet he's fantasizing," her sister said.

Gerda looked at her. "Fantasizing?"

"We're twins," Idun said, as if that were all the explanation Gerda needed.

"And?" said the navigator.

Her sister sighed. "Refsland is probably imagining what it would be like to have sex with us." Then, seeing that Gerda was still perplexed, she added, "You know...at the same time?"

Gerda realized her mouth was hanging open. She closed it. "Why do you say that?" she asked.

"It's a fairly common daydream among human males," said Idun. "You've never heard of it?"

"No," said Gerda, uncomfortable with her ignorance. "I haven't. But why would anyone want to have sex with two people at once? Wouldn't it be dangerous?"

"Only among Klingons," Idun noted.

Gerda frowned. "Right. Stupid of me."

Humans had a significantly gentler sex life than Klingons did—Gerda and her sister being notable exceptions to that rule. Having been raised on the Klingon homeworld by a Klingon family, their sexual hungers and behaviors had been formed in the steaming cauldron of their adopted culture—much to the chagrin of Gerda's recently adopted lover, Carter Greyhorse.

Or at least, Gerda added, that was the way he had felt at first. After a while, Greyhorse had grown accustomed to her decidedly Klingon brand of intimacy.

She glanced at Refsland again. He seemed intent on his console, where it was his job to periodically study ambient conditions against the prospect of an emergency transport. But Gerda got the impression that he was only biding his time before he snuck another peek at her and her sister.

The navigator felt a hot lump of anger lodge in her throat. It wasn't the notion that Refsland wanted to have sex with her that bothered her so much. It was the idea that he coveted her only because she was a twin.

Without meaning to, she expressed the thought out loud.

"I know," said Idun, though she didn't sound particularly resentful. "It's as if we're a matched set of *bat'leths,* valuable only because we're exactly the same."

Gerda shot another look at Refsland. He was talking to Paxton, the communications officer, and laughing about something she couldn't make out.

For their sake, Gerda hoped it wasn't what she *thought* it was.

"Besides," she pointed out, "if Refsland wants to have sex with two women at once, why does he prefer that they look alike? Wouldn't it be a more satisfying experience for him if they looked different from each other?"

Idun grunted. "One would think so. Sometimes I find humans more difficult to understand than any other species I've met—Vulcans included."

Gerda nodded in agreement. And it didn't seem to

help that she and her sister were humans themselves.

As she thought that, she noticed that Refsland was leaving the bridge. With a sigh of relief, Gerda turned back to her monitor and resumed her search for navigational hazards.

It was a job she did better than anyone else on the *Stargazer,* Idun included. So much for their being exactly the same, she reflected, putting the thought of Refsland and his irksome imagination aside.

Ensign Andreas Nikolas stopped in front of his captain's featureless, gray ready-room door and smoothed the front of his cranberry-colored uniform.

It would take a moment before the door chimed to let Picard know there was someone outside it. The ensign used that time to put himself in the right frame of mind. After all, it wasn't every day he had a private meeting with his captain.

Nikolas just wished he had some idea what it was *about.*

Finally, the duranium surface slid aside with an audible breath of air, revealing the warm but efficient interior of Picard's ready room. As Nikolas walked inside, he saw that the captain—a man only about five years his senior— was studying some information on his computer monitor.

The ensign smiled deferentially. "You wanted to see me, sir?"

Picard turned to him and pointed to the chair on the other side of his sleek, black desk. "I did indeed, Ensign. Have a seat."

As Nikolas sat down, he saw Picard's brow crease

ever so slightly. He didn't think it was a good sign.

But what had he done to deserve a reprimand? Nothing he could think of. Then what—?

"Prior to your arrival on the *Stargazer*," the captain began abruptly, "you had a reputation for being impulsive, headstrong, and even—on occasion—insubordinate."

True, Nikolas had to concede, if only to himself. But as Picard himself had noted, that was *before* the ensign arrived on the *Stargazer.*

"It appears you earned that reputation by virtue of several well-documented arguments with Academy professors, colleagues, and superior officers."

Nikolas frowned. True again. But—

"On at least two occasions," Picard continued, "those arguments blossomed into actual fistfights."

Nikolas could feel a caustic response coming on and he stifled it. Otherwise, he would be showing the captain that the behavior he had described was still an issue.

"Permission to speak freely, sir?" he asked.

The captain sat back in his chair and nodded. "Go ahead."

Nikolas leaned forward. "With all due respect, sir, I've done my best to put all that behind me. No one has tried harder than I have to be a cooperative and productive member of this crew."

"Without question," Picard said, "you have done exemplary work here. Every officer with whom you've come in contact has attested to that fact."

The ensign didn't get it. "Then…why am I here?"

"You're here," said the captain, "because in the course of the last few weeks, you've twice been taken to sickbay with a rather spectacular collection of bruises and lacerations. And in both cases, it was the result of injuries you had suffered in the ship's gymnasium."

Again, the facts were difficult to dispute.

"Considering your penchant for getting into fights before you joined us," Picard went on, "I am concerned. If this is a step backward, I want to nip it in the bud."

The ensign shook his head. "It's not what you think, sir."

"Then what *is* it?" Picard asked.

"That first time," said Nikolas, "was when I tried to stop Ensign Caber from beating up Lieutenant Obal."

The captain's eyes narrowed. "A laudable gesture. However, Mr. Obal made it clear that he could take care of himself. One wonders why it was necessary for you to intervene."

"Sir," Nikolas rejoined, suppressing a surge of indignation, "I had no way of knowing that Obal could defend himself. I mean, he's not exactly a mountain of muscle. For all I knew, Ensign Caber was going to kill him."

Picard considered the response. "You thought you had to go to your friend's rescue. That's certainly understandable." His gaze hardened. "Or rather, it would be, if that were the only instance of this sort of behavior."

The ensign knew where the captain was going next. "You're talking about my sparring session with Lieutenant Asmund."

"I am," Picard confirmed. He tapped the screen of his computer monitor with a fingernail. "According to Doctor Greyhorse's report, at least one of the blows you took to your head was serious enough to cause you to lose consciousness."

Nikolas sighed. "I didn't expect it to go that far."

"But it *was* a sparring session. And your opponent was one of the most formidable hand-to-hand fighters on the ship."

"I know that now, sir. But at the time—"

"You had no idea. I believe that." Nonetheless, Picard seemed unimpressed. "Where there is smoke, Ensign, there is fire. And where there are fights, there is the will to engage in them."

Nikolas groped for a way to assure the captain that he wasn't going to get into any more fights. But in the end, all he could say was "It won't happen again."

The captain looked at him. "I'm glad you said that. But it doesn't set my mind at ease."

What more can I do? Nikolas wondered silently.

"If I were you," said Picard, "I would take special care to avoid physical conflicts with my colleagues— whether they start in anger or not." His features softened. "It would be a shame to mar what is becoming a most compelling case for promotion."

Nikolas found himself smiling. "Promotion, sir?"

"That's correct, Ensign. But if that's to be even a possibility, you'll have to show me that you can stay out of sickbay. Understood?"

A promotion. Nikolas nodded. "Understood, sir."

"In that case," said Picard, "you are dismissed."

"Yes, sir," the ensign responded. "Thank you, sir."

And he left the captain's ready room a lot more light-hearted than when he entered it.

* * *

Vigo packed the last of the three uniforms he intended to take planetside with him. Then he closed his gray plastic garment case, latched it, removed it from his bed, and placed it on the floor beside his bedroom door.

The *Stargazer*'s chief weapons officer took a look around his quarters and decided that everything was in order. With nothing to do until he was called down to the shuttlebay, he sat down on the room's only chair.

It was a bit too small for him. In fact, all the furniture in his quarters, indeed in the entire ship, was too small. But then, he wasn't the first Pandrilite who had been forced to overcome that problem in his dealings with other species.

As Vigo reflected on that, he heard a soft, melodic chime. Getting up from his chair, he emerged from his bedroom into the small anteroom beyond it and said, "Please come in."

The doors to the anteroom parted, revealing his friend and colleague Pug Joseph. The ship's acting security chief, Joseph, was a stocky, sandy-haired man whose straightforwardness had endeared him to the other members of the crew.

Vigo found it a refreshing quality in a species that often seemed to pride itself on its guile. Not that that was all bad. It made the humans on board some of Vigo's most challenging *sharash'di* partners.

"So," said Joseph, "all packed?"

"As a matter of fact," said Vigo, "I am."

Joseph smiled. "Boy, I envy you. I mean, going down to Wayland Prime...every weapons innovation in the last ten years has come out of that place."

Vigo couldn't argue with Joseph's assessment of the

place. The Level One Development Facility on Wayland Prime had become a veritable hotbed of innovation thanks to the handful of brilliant tactical engineers Starfleet had assembled there.

"And," Joseph added, "as if that weren't enough of a plum, you're going to be one of the first weapons officers in the fleet to see the new Type Nine emitter."

Truly, Vigo was looking forward to examining the new and improved ship's-phaser emitter, and watching it perform in test mode. But that wouldn't be the biggest thrill he was likely to encounter on Wayland Prime.

"Hey," said Joseph, "I heard the guy who spearheaded the Type Nine project is a Pandrilite. Name's Ejanix."

Vigo nodded. "Yes."

"Do you know him?"

The weapons chief smiled to himself. "As matter of fact," he said, "I do."

First Officer Gilaad Ben Zoma stood in the middle of the *Stargazer*'s shuttlebay and considered nothing.

At least, it *looked* like nothing. It was actually a transparent, semipermeable barrier that separated the atmosphere in the shuttlebay from the vacuum of space.

"So it's working all right now?" he asked.

"It's working fine," said Chiang, the shuttlebay supervisor, "as you can see."

Ben Zoma smiled. "Or not see, as the case may be."

Earlier that morning, the barrier had displayed some instability, as evidenced by the pale yellow ripples running through it. Then, about an hour ago, it had actually begun to sputter.

The last thing anyone else in the shuttlebay wanted was an unstable barrier, considering that everyone's lives depended on how well it worked. Chiang had made note of that to Ben Zoma, who had in turn made note of it to Simenon and his engineers.

The result? A new wave projector and a much more relaxed Lieutenant Chiang.

"Let me know if you have any more trouble with it," Ben Zoma advised the supervisor.

"Don't worry," said Chiang. "I will."

That promise exacted, the first officer strode across the shuttlebay and headed for the exit. He was just shy of the doors when they slid open and admitted Lieutenant Kastiigan.

"Commander Ben Zoma," he said happily. "I was told you would be down here."

"Well," said Ben Zoma, "you were told right."

Kastiigan had been with them for just a few weeks—ever since the previous science officer was relieved of her duties and sent back to Earth. In that short time, the Kandilkari had shown himself to be as canny and dedicated a science officer as anyone could have wanted.

"May I speak with you for a moment?" Kastiigan asked.

"Sure," said the first officer. "I've got nothing urgent at the moment. What is it?"

The science officer lifted his chin. "I understand Lieutenant Vigo is going to attend a meeting on Wayland Prime."

"That's true," Ben Zoma told him. "They're demonstrating a new generation of phaser technology for Vigo and a few other weapons officers."

"I don't suppose there is any possibility of danger there?" Kastiigan asked.

Ben Zoma was surprised by the question. "I don't think so. Why do you ask?"

The Kandilkari shrugged. "I just want you to know that if there was a possibility of danger, I would be perfectly willing to attend the demonstration with Lieutenant Vigo."

The first officer smiled at the notion. "You mean as his bodyguard?"

"If you like. I just find the idea of our weapons officer facing some serious danger on his own a bit disturbing."

"As would I," Ben Zoma said. "That is, if there *were* any serious danger—which there isn't."

"Yes," said Kastiigan. "You mentioned that."

"So there's really no need for a bodyguard," the first officer added, just to make sure there was no confusion.

"Apparently not," said the Kandilkari.

The room was silent for a moment. Ben Zoma felt compelled to throw some sound into it.

"Is there anything else?" he asked.

"Nothing," the science officer assured him. "Thank you for your time, Commander."

"No problem," said Ben Zoma.

But as Kastiigan left him standing there in the shuttlebay, he found himself wondering just what in blazes they had been talking about.

Ensign Cole Paris couldn't help liking the way things were turning out.

He liked the fact that he had come to grips with his

chronic anxiety problem, born of trying to live up to the illustrious Paris name. He liked the trust Captain Picard had begun to place in him, making him the number-two helm officer on the ship behind the amazing Idun Asmund.

And he liked the fact that Second Officer Wu had decided to remain on the *Stargazer,* instead of returning to her old ship for the sake of a promotion.

Having Wu around gave Paris a comfort level he had never enjoyed before—not just since he had graduated from the Academy, but *ever.* It gave him the confidence to take on any challenge that came his way, and on a ship like the *Stargazer* they came his way all the time.

Paris was even getting used to Nikolas, his roommate. The guy wasn't much for neatness or discipline, and he was a little too preoccupied sometimes with the opposite sex, but he did everything the senior staff officers expected of him—and more, if he could.

And if Paris needed a hand with something, he was sure that Nikolas would give it to him. There was something to be said for that as well.

At that particular moment, Paris was on his way to the bridge to give someone *else* a hand. Lieutenant Asmund had asked him to recalibrate the helm controls on one of the *Stargazer*'s shuttlecraft. Normally, that would have been a job for Lieutenant Chiang's people in the shuttlebay, but Lieutenant Asmund was going to have to use the shuttle soon and she preferred that Paris take care of it.

It was quite a compliment, the ensign mused. Of course, Lieutenant Chiang might not think so. In fact—

Before he could complete his thought, he realized he

was about to bump into something. His reflexes taking over, he sidestepped the object.

It was only after he took stock of his surroundings that he realized it wasn't an *object* he had avoided. Or rather, it wasn't *just* an object.

It was Ensign Jiterica, inside the Starfleet standard-issue containment suit she was forced to wear in order to operate as a member of the crew.

Unlike anyone else on the *Stargazer,* Jiterica was a Nizhrak—a low-density being whose species developed in the upper atmosphere of a gas giant. In her natural state, she was a cloud of ionic particles larger than the confines of the ship's bridge. Hence, the containment suit, which allowed her to interact with the rest of the crew and fit into the same spaces they did.

Unfortunately, the suit was awkward for Jiterica to move. Even something as simple as standing up or sitting down was a difficult and complex maneuver. On top of that, the suit was a bulky item that took up more room than most of the ensign's fellow crewmen.

Which occasionally made her a target for someone who wasn't watching where he was going.

Paris looked through Jiterica's faceplate, where he could see a ghostly female countenance. The Nizhrak was getting better at simulating a human face, he noted. A *lot* better.

"I'm sorry," he said earnestly. "I didn't see you coming."

What appeared to be a smile took hold of the Nizhrak's face. "It's all right," Jiterica said in the mechanical voice the suit allowed her. "I'm not injured."

Funny, thought Paris. The technology in the suit didn't permit inflection. And yet Jiterica seemed to have found a way to impose a tone on her voice.

A rather pleasant tone, at that.

He found himself smiling back at her. "It's a good thing I wasn't this clumsy that day in the shuttle. Otherwise we never would have rescued the *Belladonna*."

Paris was, of course, referring to the research vessel the *Stargazer* had encountered a couple of weeks earlier. Caught in a cosmic sinkhole, the *Belladonna* and her crew were slowly but surely slipping away.

But Paris and Jiterica, working together, gave the research ship a chance at survival. And in the end, that was all the *Belladonna* needed.

Paris remembered how good it felt to know he'd had a part in saving all those scientists. And he remembered also how close he had felt to Jiterica, whose life had been in his hands.

He didn't know why he hadn't seen much of Jiterica after that, but he regretted the oversight. He had liked that feeling of closeness. He didn't want to lose it.

"You're not clumsy," she told him. "I'm the clumsy one." And she used an arm of the suit to point to its chest.

"Anyone would be clumsy if they had to walk around in that suit all day," he said.

Jiterica's expression seemed to falter then, and he was afraid that he had insulted her. But a moment later, the smile returned to her face.

"It *is* difficult," she said. "I just didn't think anyone here understood that."

Paris shrugged. "I think we all do. We just don't say it."

Jiterica looked at him. *"You did."*

And the expression behind her faceplate changed again. But this time, it didn't seem to falter. If anything, it grew stronger and more distinct—especially the eyes.

They seemed to reach right into him, even more so than a pair of human eyes might have.

That's when Paris remembered that he had someplace to go. "I'd like to stay and talk," he said, "but I'm due in the shuttlebay. But...maybe we can get together some other time."

Jiterica's head seemed to tilt a little behind her faceplate. "Some other time," she echoed.

Paris looked at her a moment longer. Then he made his way past her and headed for the turbolift.

But as he came to a bend in the corridor, he turned back...and saw that she was still standing there where he had left her, watching him go. It pleased him that it was so, though at the time he couldn't have said why.

Admiral Arlen McAteer leaned back in his plastiform chair and considered the slightly convex screen of his desktop monitor, where a swarm of tiny, bright-red dots were scattered as if at random over a stark green-on-black grid.

The grid represented the sector of the Alpha Quadrant for which the admiral and the captains assigned to him were responsible. The tiny red dots stood for the Starfleet vessels commanded by those captains.

There was a great deal going on these days in McAteer's sector. A great deal of unrest among the various species residing there. A great deal of posturing and finger-pointing and secret deal-making.

Like any admiral worth his salt, McAteer recognized these maneuverings for what they were—a prelude to armed conflict. It was the obvious conclusion. All the classic signs were there.

McAteer had already distinguished himself many times over the course of his Starfleet career. He wouldn't have become an admiral otherwise.

But if he could forestall what was shaping up to be a fair-sized war with repercussions in the Alpha Quadrant and beyond, it would make his other accomplishments pale by comparison. It would be his signature achievement, the one that cadets would study at the Academy for hundreds of years to come.

All he would have to do was head off the harbingers of the conflict one by one. But it wouldn't be easy. He would need to use all the resources at his disposal and deploy them with surgical precision.

Fortunately for McAteer, he was blessed with a cadre of veteran captains, men and women whose judgment had been tested time and again under the most dangerous and demanding circumstances. The officers in command of the admiral's vessels were among the most experienced in the fleet.

With one notable exception.

Sighing, McAteer tapped out a command on his keyboard. The image on his screen changed, its grid and its swarm of red dots giving way to a white-stars-and-laurel-leaf design on a field of startling blue.

The Federation insignia. It was what came up on the

admiral's monitor whenever he started to compose a subspace message to one of his subordinates—in this case, the green apple he would have dearly loved to replace with an older and more seasoned officer.

McAteer still hoped to do that. But for the time being, he was embroiled in the most complex card game of his career, and he had to play the hand he had been dealt.

Leaning forward in his chair, the admiral said, "Good day, Captain. I trust this communication finds you well. By the time you receive it, you will have dropped off your weapons officer at Wayland Prime and should be awaiting new orders. Well, here they are.

"You're to proceed to the Mara Zenaya system, where our long-range scans have revealed the appearance of a peculiar anomaly—one that wasn't there the last time we surveyed the system, and may not be there indefinitely. You're to examine this anomaly close-up, record your findings, and transmit them back to us here on Earth."

McAteer frowned. "I know what you're thinking. Why send a *Constellation*-class starship on what appears to be a simple scientific survey mission? As it happens, this may turn out to be *more* than a simple survey mission—since Mara Zenaya is situated on what appears to be the edge of Balduk territory."

Every captain in the sector was familiar with the Balduk—a fiercely proud and intensely territorial species with whom Federation vessels had clashed on more than one occasion. Any captain would also know that the Balduk had a propensity for "creative" charting when it came to the boundaries of their designated space.

"The Balduk haven't yet come out and said that they

own the anomaly," said McAteer, "but my guess is that they will do so just as soon as we show up. That's been their modus operandi since our first contact with them. As soon as they see something of value to someone else, they figure it should be of value to them too.

"So you're going to have to perform a balancing act. We don't want to get into a knock-down-drag-out with the Balduk, but we also don't want to lose a chance to study this anomaly."

The admiral smiled. "Good luck, Captain. I look forward to hearing all about it. McAteer out."

Tapping out another command, he ended the message. *There,* he thought. *That ought to do it.*

Normally, he wouldn't have been concerned about the outcome of such an assignment—a walk in the park, really, compared with the missions most of his captains were embarking on these days. But then, it wasn't just any captain he was dispatching to the Mara Zenaya system.

It was Jean-Luc Picard.

Second Officer Elizabeth Wu found the *Stargazer*'s chief engineer just where the computer had said he would be—in an echo-laden Jefferies tube that led to the forwardmost part of the ship's saucer section.

There, bolted directly onto the *Stargazer*'s tritanium skeleton, was the forward tractor beam emitter—a sleek, cylindrical assembly about two meters long, with a slender, flexible conduit that allowed it to draw power from the electroplasma power grid. The emitter was surrounded by a half-dozen tiny, saucer-shaped waveguides that further secured it by tying in to the ship's structural integrity field.

Nothing on the *Stargazer* was anchored more securely—not even the warp nacelles. But then, a tractor load could place an enormous amount of stress on a tractor emitter—enough to tear it loose from the ship's spaceframe if measures weren't taken to prevent such an occurrence.

Chief Engineer Phigus Simenon was a Gnalish, a gray, scaly creature slightly shorter than she was, with a long snout, startling red eyes, and a tail that swayed back and forth as he walked.

At the moment, of course, he wasn't walking at all. He was lying on his back under the forward emitter, using a hydrospanner to open its outer casing.

Wu didn't know if Simenon was fixing a problem or anticipating one, but he was clearly engrossed in his work—so much so that he didn't even glance her way as she crawled toward him, personal access display device in hand.

"I see you're busy," she observed.

"As always," he muttered in his harsh, sibilant voice.

"Well," said Wu, "I won't take up much of your time. I was just wondering if you could shed some light on something for me—specifically, this subspace message from an Administrator Haywood."

"Haywood?" he echoed. "Don't know him."

"He seems to know *you*," said Wu. "In fact, he's sent a note of commendation to Captain Picard."

Simenon twisted his head around to regard her with his ruby red eyes. "A note—?"

"From the Federation colony on Setlik Three. Apparently," said Wu, "the engineer there is a friend of yours."

19

Understanding dawned on the Gnalish's lizardlike face. "Chiidasi. Moraal Chiidasi."

"It seems this Chiidasi fellow served with you on one of your previous assignments—the *Onjata*, I believe?"

Simenon's grunt confirmed it.

"He must have thought quite highly of you," Wu continued, "because when he had some trouble with the colony's power source, you're the one he contacted."

The engineer shrugged his narrow shoulders. "Their matter-antimatter generator was a lot like the warp engine on the *Onjata*. He knew I was familiar with it, that's all."

"That was one reason," Wu agreed. "The other was that he considered you—" She held up her padd and read from it. " 'The best engineering mind in all of Starfleet.' That's rather high praise, Mr. Simenon."

He dismissed the notion with a flip of his scaly hand. "That's just Chiidasi showing his gratitude."

The second officer smiled to herself. "No doubt. Anyway, I thought you would want to know."

"Thanks," said Simenon. Then, without any further ado, he went back to his work.

Wu shook her head. Her colleague was quite the interesting character. If his manners were anywhere near as highly developed as his engineering instincts, he would have been the most cultured individual in the fleet.

As it was, she gathered, he was just its best engineer.

From space, Wayland Prime looked to Vigo like most M-class planets, a ragged curtain of clouds partially obscuring an incredibly slow and complex dance of land and water.

Even more complex—but a lot less noticeable through the starboard observation port of Vigo's shuttle—was the unusual network of magnetic storms that laced Wayland Prime's upper atmosphere.

The storm layer served as a natural security system for the Level One Development Facility, making it impossible to transport from the *Stargazer* to the planet's surface. After all, the last thing Starfleet wanted was to make the secrets of its weapons technology easy pickings for enemies and opportunists, and the galaxy seemed to contain a surfeit of both.

Unfortunately, the storm layer also made communication with anyone off-planet an uncertain proposition. Only during the occasional lull in magnetic activity could a voice or data signal punch through to the outside universe.

"It might get a little bumpy here," said Idun Asmund, the *Stargazer*'s primary helm officer, as she made some adjustments in the shuttlecraft's attitude. "But it shouldn't be anything we can't handle."

"That's good to hear," said the weapons chief.

Idun's warning turned out to be a timely one. The shuttle began to bounce as if it were hitting one solid object after another. It went on like that for a minute or so, jolt after jolt. Then the ride began to flatten out.

By that time, they were diving through the bottom of the cloud layer and heading for the barely visible northernmost continent, a massive spiral with a spine of high mountains that boasted one of the few patches of fertile green on the entire globe. Idun made a small course adjustment and pulled the shuttle toward the innermost part of the spiral.

Vigo watched as the clouds thinned and then fled altogether, leaving him with an unobscured view of his destination. That was when he caught sight of it—the dark, U-shaped building where some of the Federation's greatest engineering minds labored to improve Starfleet's existing array of tactical options.

And one of those minds belonged to Ejanix. It was hard for Vigo to believe—and not because Ejanix's brilliance had ever been the least bit in question. It was simply that university instructors on a world like Pandril seldom rose to interstellar prominence.

Vigo laughed softly to himself. *Not seldom,* he thought. *Never.*

Idun glanced back over her shoulder at him. "Did you say something?" she asked.

"No," the weapons chief replied. "Nothing. I was just thinking of something humorous."

Humorous indeed, he added silently. The first time he met Ejanix, he had been a university student and Ejanix a fledgling instructor. It was clear to Vigo from the first day of school that his new teacher was someone special—someone brighter and more dedicated than his colleagues.

But no matter how bright Ejanix might have been, no matter how dedicated, no one had expected him to receive an invitation to teach on Earth.

Nonetheless, that is what happened. A man named Onotoyo, who was retiring as Starfleet Academy's tactical-engineering expert, was asked to make a list of recommendations as to his replacement.

He gave only one name—that of a university teacher on Pandril who had published a monograph on cutting recharge times in phaser batteries. Before Ejanix knew it, he was being wined and dined by the head of the Academy, who entreated him to move to San Francisco and become a member of the most prestigious faculty in the Federation.

Of course, Vigo reflected, the Vulcans might have taken exception to that honorific. In any case, Ejanix accepted the position—which put him in a position to instruct Vigo a second time when Vigo was accepted into the Academy.

And no educator was ever happier to see a former student. Ejanix was waiting for Vigo in his dormitory room when he arrived, defying any number of unwritten rules against professor-student fraternization. And he stayed there for hours, discussing everything from the deficiencies of *Niagara*-class propulsion systems to his travails in trying to replicate traditional Pandrilite delicacies.

Had Ejanix been less prized by the Academy, he might have been reprimanded. As it was, the institution seemed willing to look the other way.

In later years, Vigo came to understand the intensity of Ejanix's friendship. Vigo himself had always wanted to join Starfleet and see the galaxy. He had looked outward to the stars, seeing his future there.

Ejanix, on the other hand, had only aspired to be a university instructor. He hadn't ever envisioned a time when he might leave Pandril and live on some other world. As a result, he wasn't prepared for the loneliness, the cultural isolation, the lack of the familiar in everyday existence.

So when Vigo showed up at the Academy—not just a fellow Pandrilite but someone Ejanix had actually known and taught—Ejanix latched on to him the way a drowning man might latch on to a buoyant *kyerota* sac.

Over the years Vigo spent at the Academy, the urgency of Ejanix's need for companionship diminished. But at the same time, the two Pandrilites developed a truer friendship—one based on mutual respect and affection.

Meanwhile, Vigo managed to become one of Ejanix's best students, thriving on his professor's enthusiasm and innovative thinking. When honors were handed out in tactical engineering, Vigo was seldom very far down the list.

The last time he had seen Ejanix was at his graduation from the Academy. By that time, Vigo had already earned a berth on the *Gibraltar* patrolling the outskirts of Federation space in the vicinity of the Romulan Neutral Zone.

He and his mentor had sworn to keep in touch afterward, and for a while they had kept that promise via subspace packet. But in time, Vigo's resolve had thinned and apparently so had Ejanix's, and even their occasional correspondence was put off in favor of more pressing concerns.

For the last two years, Vigo and Ejanix hadn't communicated at all. But the weapons chief had heard about his old instructor's transfer to the facility on Wayland Prime and his subsequent work on the Type Nine project.

Despite the two-year lapse in their friendship, Vigo had no doubt that Ejanix would be glad to see him. They would pick up right where they had left off. Maybe Vigo would even have time to teach his mentor the game of *sharash'di*.

He recalled the look of joy and relief on Ejanix's face

that first night at the Academy, and—despite himself—
the weapons chief had to laugh again.

"Nothing again?" asked Idun, not even bothering to
turn around this time.

"Nothing again," Vigo confirmed.

Abruptly, the communications monitor came alive on
the shuttle's control console. The face that appeared on
it belonged to a woman with a dark complexion and
long, black hair drawn into a braid.

"This is Chief Echevarria," she said, "of installation
security. You're cleared to land."

"Acknowledged," said Idun.

Moments later, she set the shuttle down on an open flat
embraced by the U-shaped complex. "Enjoy your stay,"
she told the Pandrilite as she triggered the mechanism
that opened the hatch, letting in the eminently breathable
air of Wayland Prime. "I'm sure it will be stimulating."

"No doubt," said Vigo. He smiled at her. "I'll tell you
all about it when you pick me up."

"I look forward to it," said the helm officer, without
the slightest hint of irony in her voice.

Vigo wrested his garment container from the aft storage
compartment. Then he ducked to avoid the upper threshold of the hatch and stepped out onto the native ground
cover, which was short, wiry, and blue-green in color.

The sky overhead was pale blue in spots and cloud-
covered in others, the temperature cool and the humidity
high. It was like Vigo's home on Pandril at the height of
summer, the only season when temperatures were con-
sistently above freezing.

As the weapons officer closed the hatch behind him,

he saw a door open in the middle of the U shape. A figure in a black jumpsuit emerged from it. It wasn't Ejanix; his Pandrilite stature would have given him away.

Vigo's welcomer, a slim, black-and-white-striped Dedderac, inclined his head as he approached. "Welcome to Wayland Prime," he said in a slightly nasal voice. "I'm Riyyen, one of the engineers who labor here—and incidentally, the administrator of the place."

"Lieutenant Vigo of the *Stargazer.*"

Riyyen smiled. "Yes, I know. You're the only Pandrilite on the guest list." He indicated the door he had come from with a tilt of his head. "Come on. I'll show you your quarters."

"Thank you," said Vigo.

He was a bit disappointed that Ejanix hadn't been able to meet him. But then, his mentor was probably busy elsewhere in the complex—perhaps with some refinement of the Type Nine.

With a wave to Idun, he let her know he was good to go. A moment later, she took the shuttle back up.

Vigo watched it go for a moment. Then he followed Riyyen into the development facility.

Chapter Two

CAPTAIN JEAN-LUC PICARD gazed at the Mara Zenaya system, a large red dot on the black-and-green grid of his desktop monitor screen. Then he looked back at his first officer, Gilaad Ben Zoma, who was peering over Picard's shoulder to study the screen at the same time.

The man's dark, Mediterranean eyes were smiling even if the rest of his face was not. But then, Ben Zoma wasn't exactly the doom-and-gloom type.

"Interesting, isn't it?" asked the captain.

"To say the least," said his first officer. "With all the jockeying for power going on in this sector, with all the noise coming from the Cardassians and the Ubarrak and who knows who else…you would think the *Stargazer* would be assigned to deal with at least some of the repercussions."

"Yes," Picard chimed in. "Just like every other starship between here and the Beta Quadrant."

"But no," said Ben Zoma. "In his infinite wisdom, Admiral McAteer has decided to send the *Stargazer*—and only the *Stargazer*—on a scientific mission." He sat down beside the captain on a stretch of polished, black desk. "Coincidence? I don't think so."

Picard leaned back in his chair. "Clearly, I'm not the admiral's favorite captain."

Of course, he and Ben Zoma had arrived at that conclusion some time ago. Weeks earlier, McAteer had attempted to discredit Picard by pitting him against the White Wolf, an elusive and seemingly unbeatable foe.

Had it not been for Cortin Zweller, an old friend of Picard, the captain would never have known of the admiral's agenda. But Zweller had alerted the captain to McAteer's distrust of him—a product, apparently, of his age and inexperience.

Picard frowned. It wasn't easy being the youngest officer ever to command a starship.

Fortunately, he had Admiral Mehdi in his corner. It was Mehdi who had placed Picard in the center seat after the death of Daithan Ruhalter, Picard's predecessor.

Mehdi hadn't let himself be deterred by the fact that Picard was only twenty-eight years old, or that he had never had a chance to serve in the capacity of first officer. The admiral had made his choice despite all that.

But from McAteer's point of view, Picard was too inexperienced to take on such a tricky assignment. And apparently, he wasn't alone in that regard. There were officers at every level who questioned Picard's fitness to do his job.

At first, the expressions of doubt had bothered him. Now he found he was getting accustomed to them.

"Unfortunately," the captain said out loud, "there is nothing I can do about Admiral McAteer. He *is* my superior. He can have me deliver flowers if that's what he wants."

"And probably will," Ben Zoma returned, "if he thinks it'll keep you out of the limelight."

Picard chuckled, though he knew he was really laughing at himself. A sad state of affairs indeed.

"Well," he said, "if we're to conduct a scientific study, let's at least make the most of it. I want all department heads briefed inside and out on the phenomenon." He shrugged. "Who knows? Maybe we'll find more than McAteer expects and make a name for ourselves despite him."

"Maybe," his first officer allowed generously. "But it's not very likely."

Picard sighed. "You know, Commander, you could have lied to make me feel better."

"I could have," said Ben Zoma. "But I don't want to sully an otherwise flawless reputation. Don't forget—if the admiral gets his way and you're stripped of your rank, I'm next in line for the captain's chair."

Picard had to laugh. If there was anything McAteer would have liked less than a twenty-eight-year-old in the captain's chair, it was a twenty-*seven*-year-old like Ben Zoma. "The department heads, Gilaad. In the briefing room. Ten minutes."

"Aye, sir," Ben Zoma assured him. Then he left the captain's ready room to carry out his orders.

Picard glanced at his monitor one last time. Under different, more tranquil circumstances, he might have looked forward to a pure research mission, even enjoyed it.

Just not now, when the entire sector seemed to be balanced on a razor's edge.

Finally, with a sound of disgust, he eliminated the graphic from the screen. Then he swiveled in his chair, got up, and headed for the briefing room.

Nikolas sat down opposite Lieutenant Obal in the *Stargazer*'s mess hall and surveyed his friend's food tray. "Okay," he said, "what have we got here?"

"Roast chicken with giblet gravy," the Binderian announced proudly.

Nikolas had to wince. Obal—and apparently, every other member of his species—bore an unfortunate resemblance to a plucked chicken, as Joe Caber had often pointed out. Apparently, Obal had missed the irony when he put in his dinner order.

But then, Nikolas had been encouraging him to try a wider range of foods. Obal had simply done what he thought his friend wanted him to do.

"Great," he said. "How do you like it so far?"

Obal shrugged. "Well enough. It's not *plomeek* soup...but then, what is?"

For some reason, the Binderian's favorite dish of all those he had tried was some kind of bitter Vulcan gruel. *Go figure,* Nikolas thought.

"And what did *you* select?" asked Obal.

Nikolas looked down at his tray, where an oversized

plate contained a plentitude of assorted delicacies—most of them from Earth, but not all. "The usual," he said.

"Considering the quantity of food you eat," said Obal, "it's a wonder you're not overweight."

Nikolas had heard the remark before, though it had always been laced with a certain amount of envy. "What can I say? I've got the old Papadopoulos metabolism."

Obal tilted his head. "Papadopoulos?"

"My mother's maiden name," Nikolas explained. "Every man in her family ate like a pig and looked like he was on a starvation diet. I'm guessing that's where I got it."

"Heredity is a powerful force," Obal observed.

He said something more, but Nikolas didn't hear him. He was too distracted by the feminine figure that walked into the mess hall at that moment.

A figure often seen in duplicate on the bridge and around the ship. A figure no red-blooded man could ignore.

Nikolas wasn't sure if it was Gerda or Idun. Then he remembered that Idun had worn her hair up that day, and her sister had worn hers down.

Idun then, he told himself.

She was wearing a regulation uniform—a jacket with black pants—that seemed designed to conceal her considerable physical attributes. And yet, she looked fantastic in it.

Knowing it was rude to stare, the ensign tried to keep from looking in Idun's direction. But he couldn't help it. It was physically impossible.

She was just too beautiful.

"Nikolas?" said Obal.

Nikolas tore his gaze away from Idun long enough to glance at his friend. "What?"

"Pardon me if I am wrong, but it appears you are staring at Lieutenant Asmund."

The ensign sighed. "You're not wrong."

Obal made a face. "I was afraid you would say that. You know that you are going down a very dangerous road, do you not? A road you have traveled before?"

Nikolas nodded. "I know."

"Then you will desist?"

"I wish I could, Obal. She's just…" He shook his head ruefully. "Irresistible."

The security officer made a face. "I will have to take your word for it. As you might imagine, my people have different standards of physical beauty."

Nikolas wasn't surprised. Though he had never seen a female Binderian, he would have to guess that Idun had little in common with her.

"I might also point out," said Obal, "that Lieutenant Asmund doesn't show the same interest in *you*."

The ensign had to agree. If his last "date" with Idun was any indication, she didn't want any part of him.

Not that it mattered. He still couldn't stop looking at her, regardless of whether she looked back. He couldn't stop drinking her in with his eyes.

And he couldn't stop wondering what it would have been like if things had turned out differently between them.

* * *

Vigo surveyed the single narrow room in which he would be sleeping during his stay on Wayland Prime. It was actually smaller than his living quarters on the *Stargazer,* and that was saying something.

He didn't understand the need for economy. On a starship, space was at a premium. But on a planet with nothing but open terrain, and a dearth of sentient population...

Still, Vigo wasn't about to complain. "It looks fine," he told his guide.

Riyyen nodded. "I'm glad you like it. We were afraid it would be too cramped."

"It's not a problem," said Vigo, "I assure you."

"The other weapons officers won't be arriving for another hour or so, but feel free to look around. You needn't worry about stumbling onto anything you're not supposed to—all the sensitive areas have been locked down."

"Thank you," said Vigo.

"If there's nothing else," the Dedderac told him, "I'll see you at dinner."

"Actually," said Vigo, stopping Riyyen in his tracks, "there *is* something. Can you tell me where to find Ejanix?"

"Certainly," said the engineer. "He'd be in his lab." He tilted his head—an expression of curiosity in his species. "Have you and Ejanix met before?"

"We have," the Pandrilite told him. "In fact, we were pretty close friends for a while."

Riyyen's brow raised. "That's strange. He didn't mention anything." He shrugged. "In any case, just follow me. I'll take you to him."

"I'd appreciate that," Vigo said.

The engineer led him along a single long corridor, then turned down a second corridor. Ejanix's laboratory was the first door on the right.

"I'll leave you two to reminisce," said Riyyen, who obviously had some work of his own to attend to. Then he retreated along the same corridor.

Vigo eyed the closed door of Ejanix's lab. It seemed unlikely that his friend had failed to mention him. Maybe Riyyen just hadn't received the information.

Yes, he thought, that must be it.

Touching the metal plate beside the door, Vigo waited for a response. It was slow in coming—so much so that he began to wonder if Riyyen hadn't led him to an empty lab by mistake.

Then, just as Vigo was about to give up, the door slid open and revealed the room beyond it—a small, bright enclosure full of computer consoles and monitor screens. It wasn't until the weapons officer stepped inside that he saw a large, black-garbed figure huddled over one of the consoles, staring at the screen on top of it.

There was no question that it was Ejanix. Even if it weren't for the fact of the engineer's size, Vigo would still have recognized him.

Either Ejanix hadn't heard him come in or he was in the middle of some important calculation, because he didn't so much as turn his head to acknowledge his friend's presence. And Vigo, reluctant to interrupt Ejanix's work, didn't say anything either. He just stood there, waiting.

Finally, Ejanix spoke to him. But he didn't turn away from his monitor screen. "You're here," he said.

Just that. Nothing more.

"If you're busy," Vigo told him, "I can come back later."

"I *am* busy," said Ejanix. "Too busy to play host. But Starfleet Command insisted that I do so, and I never argue with Starfleet Command."

He sounded...bitter, Vigo thought. And as far as he could remember, Ejanix had never sounded bitter.

Then, unexpectedly, the engineer swiveled in his chair and faced the weapons officer. But he wasn't the Ejanix whom Vigo had known back on Earth. This Ejanix was on edge, nervous-looking, bereft of all the considerable warmth and enthusiasm he had shown in the past.

"Is everything all right?" Vigo asked.

His mentor frowned. "Frankly, it's far from all right. It's too soon for me to be talking about the Type Nine. I haven't finished testing it yet. I haven't put it through its paces. And instead of doing that, I'll be entertaining you and your counterparts from the *Essex* and the *New Orleans*."

Vigo didn't know what to say. What he finally settled for was "If I had known that a demonstration was premature, I would have turned down the invitation."

Ejanix harrumphed. "You didn't have a choice in the matter. Don't you know that yet? When Starfleet Command tells you to go somewhere, you go."

There was silence between them for a moment. It was an uncomfortable silence, too.

Vigo was the one who finally broke it. "I'm told the other weapons officers won't be here for approximately an hour. Why don't I leave you alone until then, so you can take some time to compose yourself?"

Ejanix looked away from him, as if even the sight of

him made the engineer uncomfortable. "That's kind of you," he said. "I'll see you later."

"At dinner," Vigo suggested.

"Yes," said Ejanix. "At dinner." But he didn't exactly sound as if he were looking forward to it.

Carter Greyhorse took his duties as chief medical officer quite seriously—most of the time.

At this particular moment, however, he was engaged in the sort of activity not envisioned by the architects of the *Stargazer*'s sickbay. One of his colleagues, with whom he happened to be fiercely and hopelessly in love, was pinning him against the bulkhead behind his desk—her lips pulled back from her perfect, white teeth, her fingernails etching lines of hot, fiery pain in his face, neck, and chest.

And to that point, Greyhorse had loved every second of it.

"What if someone walks in?" he asked softly, as Gerda gnawed on his lower lip.

"Then I'll hear them," she assured him. "I was trained as a warrior, remember?"

The doctor took comfort in the knowledge that Gerda didn't want their affair made public any more than he did. Relationships between officers were frowned on in Starfleet. If Captain Picard found out about them, he would be forced to recommend a transfer for one of them.

Hence, the need for secrecy—even from Gerda's sister, Idun, with whom she shared every other detail of her life. It was a need that ruled their lusts most of the time.

But their schedules had kept them apart of late, and Gerda always found it difficult to be denied.

Almost as much as Greyhorse himself did.

Still, it made him nervous to carry on like this in his office, with its transparent walls. But he didn't dare let Gerda know *how* nervous. After all, she was a warrior, as she had said, and she expected no less of her lover.

If the doctor appeared too worried, Gerda would interpret it as weakness. And nothing put a damper on a Klingon-style love affair like a perception of weakness in the male.

"Tell me," the navigator said in a husky whisper, "have you ever had a fantasy about me and my sister?"

He looked at her, surprised. "A fantasy?"

"You know...a sexual fantasy."

Greyhorse hadn't had any such thing. But even if he had, he would never have admitted it to Gerda.

"Of course not," he said.

She made a sound of triumph. "I didn't think you had. So Idun was wrong. All humans are *not* alike."

The satisfaction Gerda derived from this conclusion seemed to further ignite her ardor. Her nails dug deeper into Greyhorse's flesh, under his jacket where a couple of scratches wouldn't be noticed. Her lips pulled back even further and her breath came a little faster.

"I have to be on the bridge in a few minutes," she said. "But if I didn't..." She let her voice trail off suggestively.

Suddenly, Ben Zoma's voice flooded Greyhorse's office, turning the doctor's blood to ice. It was only after he looked around and saw that the first officer himself wasn't anywhere in evidence that Greyhorse realized the voice had issued from the intercom system.

"Yes...?" he managed in response.

"The captain would like to see the senior staff in the briefing room," said Ben Zoma. "Ten minutes."

The doctor forced himself to breathe. "I'll be there," he assured the first officer.

"Good. Ben Zoma out."

Greyhorse looked at Gerda. Despite her warrior's poise, she too looked to have been startled by the intercom message. It gave him some satisfaction that he wasn't the only one.

"Looks like you'll have to leave sooner than you thought," he told her.

"So it does," she said.

"Gerda?" said Ben Zoma, his voice ringing through sickbay a second time.

Her gaze hardened as she once more became the dutiful navigator. "Aye, sir?"

"The captain wants to see the senior staff in the briefing room. Ten minutes."

"Acknowledged," said Gerda.

"Thanks. Ben Zoma out."

Greyhorse let out a breath. "I suppose we should leave sickbay separately. We don't want to give anyone any ideas."

Gerda nodded. "I'll go first. The captain will expect me to be there early."

"As usual," said the doctor.

His lover kissed him hard on the mouth. Then, without another word, she turned and left his office.

Greyhorse watched her stride across sickbay and heaved a sigh. His heart was still pounding from the shock of hearing Ben Zoma's voice, but Gerda looked as if nothing unusual had happened.

Her gait was that of a woman of confidence. A warrior, as she had said moments earlier. And the doctor? He was different from her. He was just a man.

And not a very brave man at that.

Chapter Three

PICARD LOOKED AROUND the briefing room table and scanned the faces of his officers, whom he had just apprised of their mission to Mara Zenaya.

"Any questions?" he asked.

"Just one," asked Paxton, the communications chief. "What do we do if the Balduk show up?"

Picard had given that some thought. "If they show up," he said, "we attempt to discuss the matter with them. With luck, we'll be able to negotiate a reasonable outcome."

Knowing the Balduk as they did, his officers looked skeptical. The captain didn't blame them.

"But if negotiations fail," he continued, "we will not fight them. We will withdraw."

He didn't like the notion of retreat any better than his officers did. However, it didn't make sense to risk the lives of his crew for the sake of nonessential research, and research was the only thing at stake there.

There weren't any colonies to protect in that part of space, or claims to assert. Just the anomaly.

"Which makes it all the more important," said Ben Zoma, "to gather our data quickly and efficiently. That way, we know we won't walk away empty-handed."

There were nods around the table. Clearly, Ben Zoma's comment had infused them with a sense of resolve.

"If there is nothing else," said Picard, "you are dismissed. But keep me posted on your preparations."

Again, there were nods. And on that decidedly positive note, the meeting ended.

Vigo arrived at the mess hall at precisely the time posted on the installation's computer net. But as he looked around at the half-dozen round, black plastic tables in the room, he saw that some of them were already occupied.

In fact, he counted almost twenty individuals, both male and female, representing nearly as many species. He couldn't help noticing that Ejanix wasn't among them.

On the other hand, the other two weapons officers seemed to have arrived. Vigo could tell because they were the only ones in the room—besides him, of course—who were wearing standard-issue Starfleet uniforms.

One of the weapons officers was a human, a lanky fellow with a square jaw and a receding hairline. The other was a Vobilite, as evidenced by his mottled red skin and the curved tusks that protruded from either side of his mouth.

Vigo had barely made the observation when he found

Riyyen beside him with a tray in his hands. "I see you found your way," said the engineer. "Come on, I'll introduce you to your fellow ship officers."

Vigo allowed the Dedderac to escort him across the room. As he did so, the weapons officers looked up at them.

Indicating the newcomers with a sweep of his black-and-white striped hand, Riyyen said, "Lieutenant Vigo of the *Stargazer,* this is Lieutenant Sebring of the *Essex* and Lieutenant Runj of the *New Orleans.*"

"Good to meet you," said Sebring, getting up and extending his hand. "How's life on the *Stargazer?*"

"Fine," said Vigo, engaging in the handclasp so highly valued by humans.

"Do you mind if we sit down?" asked Riyyen, as polite as any other Dedderac of Vigo's acquaintance.

"Not at all," said Runj, his words slurred by the impediment posed by his tusks.

The Pandrilite decided he could wait to get his food. It wasn't often that he got the chance to speak with other chief weapons officers.

"So," said Sebring, shooting Vigo a conspiratorial smile, "what's the deal with that twenty-eight-year-old captain? I forget his name."

"His name is Picard," said Vigo.

"That's right, Picard. Are you okay with him?"

The Pandrilite sighed. "I am quite pleased. Whatever his age, he is the finest officer I have ever known."

"High praise," Runj observed.

"Of which he is eminently deserving," Vigo said.

"Well," said Sebring, "it's good to hear all that scuttlebutt about him is unfounded. Have you had a chance to see the Type Nine yet?"

"Not yet," Vigo told him.

"I can't wait," said Sebring. He turned to Riyyen. "Any idea when we'll get our demonstration?"

"It's scheduled for tomorrow morning," said the Dedderac. "I can't say what time exactly."

"Funny," said Sebring, grinning as he looked around the mess hall. "You engineers are pretty precise when it comes to dinnertime. I'm surprised you don't know *exactly* when the demonstration is."

Riyyen smiled politely. "I might, Lieutenant, if I were the engineer in charge of the Type Nine project." He glanced apologetically at Vigo. "The one who *is* in charge of it tends to be a bit eccentric lately, not to mention significantly less interested in mealtimes than the rest of us."

The Pandrilite had already experienced Ejanix's newfound eccentricity, so the information didn't catch him off guard. Nonetheless, he found it disturbing.

Ejanix had always been a gregarious individual, if not especially adept at social encounters. Vigo would have guessed his mentor to be among the first to report for dinner. And yet, Riyyen seemed to have observed otherwise.

Clearly, Ejanix had changed in the time he had spent on Wayland Prime. Vigo just wished he knew why.

Wutor Qiyuntor had shamed both himself and the blood that ran through his Balduk veins.

First, more than a year earlier, he had lost a large portion of the land his ancestors had left him—all the fertile, productive, and profitable terrain west of the

Sjadjok River. There were those who said it was not his fault—that the arbiter had been bribed by Clan Osyelodth to rule in their favor, or that it was Wutor's father whose mismanagement had opened the door to Osyelodth's claim.

But Wutor hadn't embraced the excuses offered to him. As far as he was concerned, the loss was his—along with the humiliation that accompanied it.

Then, a mere few months ago, he had made a critical error—and in an infinitely more serious arena than the land arbiter's court. Wutor had been serving as commander of the *Ssakojhin,* a High Order war vessel with an unblemished tradition of victory, when an alien ship-pack violated a new Balduk boundary.

The *Ssakojhin* and her subordinate vessels were sent to turn back the aliens. However, they were more powerful than the overseers of the High Order had imagined.

Wutor's battle with the invaders had barely gotten under way when he lost the first of his subordinate vessels. Two more followed in short order, and the *Ssakojhin* suffered near-crippling damage trying to preserve the rest.

It was only because reinforcements appeared that Wutor and his crew survived, and that the aliens were finally driven off. Had his rescuers shown up even a few minutes later, the *Ssakojhin* and the remainder of her pack would have been destroyed.

For his failure, Wutor was removed from the *Ssakojhin* and assigned to a Middle Order vessel, the *Ekhonarid.* Again, his supporters said the failure wasn't his fault. They claimed that the overseers of the High

Order were to blame, for it was they who had underestimated the force needed to repel the invaders.

But Wutor hadn't embraced those excuses either. He had accepted his demotion without complaint, resolving to redeem himself in the eyes of his superiors.

Of course, it was unlikely that he would get an opportunity to do so. Middle Order ships were seldom dispatched against enemy vessels. They were more often used as rescue or repair vehicles, their mission to preserve the effectiveness of High Order ships and their crews.

It was a bitter brew for Wutor to swallow. After all, he had been one of the Prime One's shining stars once. He had been highly regarded in both clan council and war circle.

He sighed now as he stood in the commander's brace on the bridge of the *Ekhonarid* and contemplated how far he had fallen, and how fast. And if he wasn't careful, he knew, he could plummet the rest of the way.

"Commander," said his chief mechanic, a female named Tsioveth, "the plasma conduits on the weapons deck are ready to crack. We need new ones."

Wutor looked at her, unimpressed by the scowl on her face. "We need a great *many* things."

And if he were still in command of the *Ssakojhin,* he would have gotten them. That was the way of things in the High Order. Then again, if he were still on the *Ssakojhin* he wouldn't have *needed* new plasma conduits.

Tsioveth spat. "Then I will not be responsible for the crew in the weapons enclosure. If they are steam-cooked like desert tortoises in the Prime One's cooking hole, so be it."

For the hundredth time since he took command of the *Ekhonarid,* Wutor grabbed the mechanic by the arm and drew her close to him—close enough to smell her most recent meal.

"You *will* be responsible," he snarled. "Now get back to the weapons deck and do everything in your power to keep those conduits from leaking."

It was a little game they played, he and Tsioveth. She refused to be held accountable for the ship's deficiencies, and he denied her the right to do so. Unfortunate, to be sure, but that was how it was in the Middle Order.

With a curl of her lip, the mechanic pulled her arm from Wutor's grasp. Then she slunk off the bridge into one of the descent compartments.

The commander glanced at his pilot, Jeglen, who had witnessed the exchange with Tsioveth. Apparently, Jeglen knew better than to comment on it. That was good.

After all, Wutor didn't want to have to get rid of him and look for another pilot. Experienced ones like Jeglen were too hard to come by, especially when the *Ekhonarid* was all that could be offered them.

Then again, there was such a thing as *too* much experience. No one was a better example of that than Potrepo, the *Ekhonarid*'s aged weaponer. Even at an advanced age, he was still eager to fight—but to his superior's chagrin, his accuracy didn't always match his enthusiasm.

Turning to the concave screen that filled the forward part of the bridge, Wutor regarded the stars rushing by on either side of them. At this pace, they would reach their destination in less than a day.

That is, he added mentally, *if Tsioveth can convince the plasma conduits to stay together.*

Vigo was the first to arrive at the elongated, dimly lit testing chamber where Ejanix was scheduled to demonstrate his new phaser emitter.

Even Ejanix hadn't gotten there yet. However, the weapons officer didn't mind. It gave him an opportunity to inspect the square, half-meter-thick piece of hull-quality tritanium that had been suspended at one end of the chamber.

At the other end stood a transparent enclosure with an aperture in its front wall about the size of Vigo's thumbnail. It was through that aperture that Ejanix would unleash the phaser emitter's powerful energy beam.

Overnight, Vigo had given much thought to his mentor's behavior. With the specter of armed conflict arising in the quadrant, Ejanix had no doubt been under a lot of pressure to complete his work—and that could have taken a greater toll on him than anyone anticipated.

Normally, an engineer would look forward to an opportunity to show off the fruits of his labor to a group of individuals capable of appreciating them. Ejanix's comments the night before notwithstanding, maybe he would benefit from a few compliments on the Type Nine.

Vigo sincerely hoped so. It made him uncomfortable to see his mentor in so black a mood.

"Hey, Vigo," said a voice.

The weapons officer turned and saw Sebring enter the room, Riyyen and Runj right behind him. All three of them joined Vigo at the hanging section of tritanium.

"Time for the dog and pony show," Sebring remarked.

"Actually," said Riyyen, "I have seen the Type Nine in action. It is quite impressive."

Vigo didn't doubt it. And yet, Ejanix had claimed he wasn't ready to demonstrate the Type Nine. Was that an accurate assessment, the weapons officer wondered, or merely a measure of his friend's irritability?

Before he could ponder the question more fully, Ejanix entered the room pushing a large antigrav cart. On it was a meter-long, black plastic container shaped like a Terran beehive, its two halves held together with tritanium bands.

As Vigo and the others watched, Ejanix guided the cart into the transparent enclosure. Then he locked it into place, shut off its antigrav function, and hooked it up to an EPS grid in the wall beside it.

His demeanor didn't seem to have changed appreciably from the night before. He didn't look at any of the weapons officers, even when he finally addressed them.

"I'd advise you to take your seats," he announced. "Accidents have been known to happen, and the Type Nine is aimed directly at that tritanium section."

Neither Vigo nor his colleagues had to be told twice. Depositing themselves in a row of chairs set up along one wall, they waited while Ejanix opened the magnetic locks on the black plastic container. A moment later, its two halves fell away, revealing the Type Nine.

It was more streamlined than Vigo had imagined, with rounded edges, a longer barrel, and a significantly more compact body than the Type Eight, though it retained the basic Y shape of its predecessor. But none of them had made the trip to Wayland Prime to discuss esthetics.

"The Type Nine," said Ejanix, "is a significant improvement over the Type Eight, which—as you know—has been the standard in starship design for the last dozen years. The Type Nine can produce more firepower, sustain that firepower for a longer period of time, and yet draw less plasma energy than any phaser emitter before it."

Without any further introduction, Ejanix signaled to Riyyen to dim the lights. Then, with a press of a stud on the side of the device, he activated it.

Instantly, a seething red beam no more than a couple of centimeters thick shot through the hole in the transparent cube and speared the tritanium section, creating a small cloud of vapor at the point of contact.

"At this wattage and beam width," said Ejanix, "a Type Eight would take nearly forty seconds to punch through an unshielded section of that thickness."

He had barely gotten the last word out when he reached down and deactivated the emitter, causing the beam to vanish. The weapons officers looked at one another, wondering why the demonstration had ended so abruptly.

Ejanix emerged from the transparent cubicle and walked over to the tritanium section. Then, as Riyyen brought the lights up, he guided it along a narrow ceiling rail to the part of the room where Vigo and his colleagues were sitting.

Vigo could see the hole the beam had dug into the section. It was blackened and bubbled around the edges.

"As you will see," said Ejanix, drawing a calibrated metal rod from his pocket, "the Type Nine doesn't require forty seconds to pierce a half-meter of tritanium."

Inserting the rod into the hole, he showed them all how deep it went. Then he extracted it and held it in front of Runj.

The Vobilite noted the measurement on the rod. Turning to Vigo and Sebring, he said, "Eighty-five centimeters." He glanced at Ejanix. "In what? Fifteen seconds?"

Ejanix nodded. "Approximately."

Sebring looked more than a little impressed. "What's its maximum effective tactical range?"

"Two hundred and seventy thousand kilometers," said Ejanix. "But I'm working on extending that."

The Type Nine was quite an accomplishment, Vigo reflected. But there was no hint of pride in Ejanix's voice as he described the device, no passion, no evidence that he felt even the slightest sense of achievement.

Clearly, his resentment had superseded any other emotion. The old Ejanix would never have let that happen, but this was clearly not the old Ejanix.

"And how did you make this happen?" Sebring wondered. "Did you change the timing on the switching gates? Maybe reconfigure the emitter crystal?"

"Yes and yes," Ejanix told him. "And a good deal more. I'll make the data available to you as soon as I've completed my work. Any other questions?"

How could there be? Ejanix had made it plain that he wasn't releasing any detailed information.

"In that case," he said, returning to the transparent enclosure, "I thank you for coming."

Then he packed up the Type Nine and reactivated the cart's antigrav capability. In a matter of seconds, he was guiding the device out of the cubicle.

Sebring sat back and folded his arms across his chest. "I came all this way for *that?*"

Runj scowled around his tusks. "I would have gotten more out of a subspace memo."

If Ejanix heard their complaints, he didn't respond to them. He just pushed the cart out of the room and was gone.

Vigo turned to Riyyen. The Dedderac looked embarrassed by his colleague's curtness. But if Ejanix wanted to act that way, there was nothing he could do about it.

"Well," said Sebring, "that was pretty much a waste of time. Anybody for a game of chess?"

Under different circumstances, Vigo might have suggested *sharash'di* as an alternative. However, his board was back on the *Stargazer*, and—truth be told—he didn't much feel like playing at the moment.

In a very real sense, he had lost his best friend.

Chapter Four

Captain's Log, Supplemental. We have established a position within two thousand kilometers of the anomaly and initiated sensor sweeps. It is my hope that we will have the opportunity to complete our mission and depart the Mara Zenaya system without incident.

His log entry complete, Picard got up from his desk, crossed his ready room, and walked out onto the *Stargazer*'s bridge. He had left Ben Zoma ensconced in the center seat, but the first officer was now peering over Gerda's shoulder at the monitors on her navigation console.

"How are we doing?" the captain asked them.

Ben Zoma looked up at him. "This thing is a lot more powerful than it looks."

Picard glanced at the forward viewscreen, where the anomaly—an elongated phenomenon of modest dimensions—pulsed with a gaudy violet light. "How much more powerful?"

Ben Zoma told him.

"Powerful indeed," the captain noted respectfully. "Is the *Stargazer* in any danger?"

The first officer shook his head. "I don't think so. At this distance, the shields should hold up just fine."

Picard nodded. And there wasn't any sign of the Balduk, or he would have been alerted. So far, so good.

Just as he thought that, he heard himself addressed over the intercom system. "Transporter Room One to Captain Picard."

Picard looked up at the intercom grid hidden in the ceiling. "Yes, Mr. Refsland, go ahead."

"Sir," said the operator, "a crewman just arrived on my transporter pad."

The captain glanced at Ben Zoma, who shrugged his shoulders. Obviously he didn't know any more about it than Picard did.

"I didn't order any transports," the captain noted.

"I didn't think so either, sir," said Refsland. "But here she is nonetheless."

An even more disturbing question came to mind. "Exactly where did she beam here *from,* Mr. Refsland? There aren't any vessels registering on our sensors."

He turned to his navigator just to make sure. Gerda consulted her monitors, then confirmed Picard's statement with a shrug of her own.

"That's not clear, sir," Refsland replied. "My instruments tell me she came from the direction of the anomaly. But that doesn't seem possible."

Stranger and stranger, the captain thought. All kinds of possibilities whirled in his brain.

"Are you certain this is a member of the crew?" he asked the transporter operator.

"I am indeed, sir."

"And who is it?"

A pause. "I'm not certain," said Refsland.

Picard could feel the muscles spasming in his jaw. "You're not certain?" he echoed.

"That's correct, sir."

"But you said you're *certain* she's a member of the crew."

"She is, sir."

"Then you know her."

By that point, there was a pained note in Refsland's voice. "I do, sir."

"But you're not certain who it is? I hope this isn't a joke, Mr. Refsland, because I'm not in the mood."

"It's not a joke, sir. If I can explain..."

"I wish you would," said Picard.

"I recognize her," said the transporter operator. "I just don't know *which* Lieutenant Asmund it is."

As if on cue, both Idun and Gerda turned to look at the captain. Now he was *certain* that it was a joke.

"Mr. Refsland," he said slowly, *"both* Lieutenant Asmunds are here with me on the bridge."

There was another pause. Picard wasn't surprised. Whatever bizarre and uncharacteristic jest Refsland had had in mind, he had just stymied it.

Or so the captain thought until his transporter operator spoke up again.

"I don't see how that's possible," said Refsland. "One of them is standing right here in front of me."

Picard leaned back in his chair. This had now gone beyond the parameters of a joke. Clearly, the man was trying to get his goat, for no reason the captain could discern.

But he still had to investigate Refsland's report. It was his duty as commanding officer of the *Stargazer,* regardless of how much he doubted his source's veracity.

"Security," he said.

"Joseph here," came the response.

"Go to Transporter Room One," Picard told him, "and tell me whom you see there."

It took a few minutes for the security chief to make his way to his appointed destination. In the meantime, the captain drummed his fingers on his armrest.

Finally, Joseph said, "I'm here, sir."

"Mr. Refsland is present?" Picard asked.

"He is, sir."

"Is there anyone else in the room with him?"

"There is," Joseph confirmed.

"Who is it?"

A pause. "I'm not exactly sure, sir."

The captain couldn't believe it. "You're not *sure?*"

"No, sir. It's either Idun or Gerda. But they look so much alike, I can't say which one it is."

Idun and Gerda exchanged looks of surprise and mistrust. Picard didn't blame them.

"Lieutenant," he said, "please escort that individual to the brig."

"Sir?" said Joseph.

"You heard me," the captain insisted. "To the brig."

"Aye, sir," the security chief responded. But it was clear he didn't think much of the idea.

Picard turned to Ben Zoma, who looked every bit as confused as the captain did. "Number One," said Picard, "you've got the bridge. I'm going to see what this is all about."

"I can't wait to hear the explanation," said Ben Zoma.

Neither can I, thought the captain, as he made his way aft to the turbolift.

Wutor Qiyuntor was less than a light-year from the Erechek Riheyn system and the Balduk orbital stronghold circling its fourth planet when he received a message from one of the overseers of the Middle Order.

"Abort your current mission," said the overseer, a female who was surprisingly handsome for her advanced age and station, "and head for the following coordinates."

Wutor eyed the data as it came through in a band at the bottom of the bridge's concave screen. It described a point in the recently annexed area beyond the binary star Jopter Kej.

"You will find a hole in space there," the overseer continued, "and an energetic hole at that. As you know, such things often attract the attention of our enemies. But the phenomenon is in Balduk territory."

"And Balduk territory must remain inviolate," Wutor said, making the ritual reply.

Even though the overseer couldn't hear it, his bridge crew could. Commanders had been relieved of their ships for less serious infractions than failing to comply with the ritual. On the *Ssakojhin*, he wouldn't have worried about it. But here on the *Ekhonarid*, he didn't know if he could trust his officers to keep their tongues still.

"Guard the phenomenon until a High Order squadron can arrive," said the overseer. "At that point, you will go to Erechek Riheyn and carry out your duties there."

Wutor cursed silently. The overseer's words cut, and cut deeply. Had a High Order squadron been as close to the phenomenon as Wutor's was, she would never have thought to contact him. After all, he had already demonstrated his inadequacy in battle.

"That is all," said the overseer. "Guard and defend."

"Guard and defend," the commander said in return. Then he glanced at his protocol officer. "Send a message back to the Overseer confirming that we received her orders."

"As you wish," growled the officer, a stocky male with a scar down the side of his face.

Next, Wutor turned to Jeglen. "You have the coordinates," he said. "Set a course and follow it."

"Done," said the pilot, and got to work.

Wutor turned to his screen, where he could see the stars wheeling from left to right. They didn't stop until Jopter Kej was in the center of the screen.

Somewhere in the depths of Balduk space, a squadron of High Order ships was bearing down on the same star. When they arrived, Wutor would have no choice but to return to his less-than-glorious Middle Order duties.

But until they got there, the *Ekhonarid* would be all that stood between Balduk territory and the rest of the universe. And Wutor prayed to the gods of blood and fire that the rest of the universe showed up with their weapons blazing.

Refsland and Joseph were right, Picard thought, as he peered through an electromagnetic barrier in the brig. The woman who had materialized in the transporter room looked exactly like Gerda and Idun.

En route there, the captain had checked with Refsland to make sure their visitor hadn't brought any serious diseases on board. Refsland, in turn, had inspected the logs of the transporter's biofilter, which was designed to detect and eliminate dozens of harmful organisms.

Fortunately, nothing had shown up. But that didn't mean the woman herself didn't present a danger of some sort.

"Drop the barrier," he told Joseph. "Then raise it again after I'm inside."

The security officer nodded. "Aye, sir."

A moment later, the barrier vanished and Picard entered the enclosure. The woman regarded him, but didn't say anything. Obviously, she expected him to do the talking.

Which he did. "My name is Jean-Luc Picard, the captain of this vessel." He heard a subtle buzz behind him that meant the barrier had sprung back to life. "As you might expect, I have a few questions to ask of you."

She nodded.

"Number one," he said reasonably, "how did you

come to materialize on our transporter pad, considering the fact that there's no vessel even close to being in transporter range? And number two, why do you so closely resemble my helm and navigation officers?"

The woman seemed as perplexed as he was. "I'm not sure myself," she answered in a voice that was remarkably like Gerda's and Idun's. "But I'll tell you what I know."

Gerda was certain that she looked as focused on her work as ever, her eyes moving purposefully from one of her navigation monitors to another. But then, she was working as hard as she could to give that impression.

On the inside, she was anything but purposeful and focused. She was a stormy sea of curiosity, as anyone would have been if they had just learned—if only through someone else's intercom conversation—that a woman who looked exactly like her had arrived on the ship unannounced.

At the helm console, Idun seemed purposeful and focused too. But Gerda knew that her sister was every bit as unsettled as she was, every bit as consumed with curiosity.

Until a minute ago, they had known their places in the universe. They were women, officers, Klingons by temperament if not by blood. And twins, identical to each other in almost every aspect of their being.

Now it seemed possible that at least one fact of their existence—one very important fact—might be in need of reassessment. If the woman in the brig looked the way Refsland and Joseph had described her, Gerda and Idun were no longer the only two of their kind.

Somehow, there was a *third*.

But despite what she had heard, Gerda wasn't ready to believe it—at least, not yet. First, she wanted to see the evidence with her own eyes.

Picard ignored the subtle buzz of the brig barrier and waited for the woman to respond.

"First off," she said, "my name is Asmund. I hold the rank of lieutenant on a ship called *Stargazer.*"

Stranger and stranger, the captain thought. *"This* vessel is called *Stargazer.* And I've got two Lieutenant Asmunds serving on my bridge—but you're not either one of them."

The woman absorbed the information. "And one of your officers is Pug Joseph, but not the Pug Joseph I know."

Picard frowned. "Go on."

"As to how I got here...I can only tell you I was beaming onto a ship called the *Crazy Horse,* with which we had arranged a rendezvous so I could return to Earth on personal business. The transport procedure seemed to go as it always does—except I wound up here instead of on the *Crazy Horse.*"

Picard mulled what the woman had told him. "Not a very enlightening account."

The newcomer seemed to stiffen. "With all due respect, Captain, I'm giving you the facts as I know them. If this sounds a bit strange to you, rest assured that it sounds just as strange to me."

Picard saw the look on her face—one of resentment and indignation—and wondered if he was being unnecessarily suspicious. But then, it wasn't every day another Asmund showed up on his ship.

Of course, there was an explanation at hand, if an extremely bizarre one. On at least one other occasion in Starfleet history, a seemingly routine transport had resulted in a crossing to another universe. If it could happen once, it could have happened a second time.

The captain hadn't mentioned the possibility because he wanted to hear the woman's story first. But now that he had, it was sounding more and more like she had experienced a reprise of that other ill-fated transport.

"Tell me," he said, "this *Stargazer* on which you serve...is it part of a fleet?"

"Yes," she said. "We call it a *Star*fleet. It's the military and scientific arm of a loosely organized union of planets called the Confederation."

Well, Picard reflected, *there is at least a small difference between our two universes, even if it is a matter of only a few letters.*

"And is there a dominant member in your...Confederation?" he asked.

The woman shook her head. "No. That's the whole point—that every member world is equal to all others. Some worlds are less active in the organization, but that's by choice."

It was the answer Picard had hoped to hear.

He went on to ask his guest other questions, focusing in more narrowly on interstellar politics. Judging from her responses, her universe had its share of conflicts. But for the most part, it was an orderly place with long-observed treaties and well-patrolled borders.

And no trace of tyranny, apparently. At least, not in the union called the Confederation.

Picard mulled everything the woman had said. Then he asked a question that was more to the point of his inquiry. "Have you ever heard of a man called Kirk?"

"Yes," said Lieutenant Asmund. "Why?"

"He was...my hero when I was a boy."

It was stretching the truth, to say the least. But then, he needed an explanation, and that was the first plausible one that came to mind.

The woman shrugged. "Kirk was a starship captain. A good one, too, according to the histories I've read. He died some fifty years ago, fighting Klingons in the Mutara sector."

Picard was familiar with the incident. But in his universe, Kirk had survived and gone on to play a key role in the Khitomer Conference, where the Federation and the Klingon Empire finally began to put aside their differences.

"Anything else?" asked Lieutenant Asmund. "My grandmother's recipe for oatmeal cookies, perhaps?"

The captain had to smile. "My apologies. But I have discovered, in my short tenure as commanding officer of this vessel, that people are often not what they seem. I'm forced to apply that standard to you as well."

The woman nodded. "Apology accepted. And believe me, I understand the need to be wary. But I assure you, Captain, I'm not here for any nefarious purposes. Nothing would please me more than to get back on that transporter pad and be returned to my own *Stargazer.*"

"I am sure that's true," Picard told her. "However, considering we do not know precisely how you got here, it may be a tricky matter to get you back."

The lieutenant didn't look happy with his response. "I was hoping you would say something else," she admitted, "but I can't say I'm surprised."

"I can tell you this," he said. "We will do everything in our power to return you to your place and time of origin. However, in case that endeavor takes some time—"

"Or never happens at all," she interjected fatalistically.

"In case of either of those outcomes, I invite you to make yourself as comfortable as you can here on the *Stargazer.* Though in line with my earlier comments regarding appearances, I feel compelled to supply you with a security escort."

"No problem," said Lieutenant Asmund. "He or she will be useful as a guide, if nothing else."

Picard nodded. "I am glad you see it that way."

Joseph, who was standing just outside the barrier, was the obvious choice for the woman's escort. After all, he was the highest-ranking security officer on the ship.

He had become a little too personally involved with the last visitor he was asked to guard—Serenity Santana of the mysterious Magnia colony. But with that experience under his belt, Picard was certain the security officer wouldn't allow himself to be fooled again.

"Just one other thing," the woman said. "You mentioned that there are a couple of Asmunds on your ship. Bridge officers, I believe."

"That is correct."

I'd like to meet them," the newcomer told him, "if that's all right with you."

The captain didn't see any reason to forbid it. And he *knew* that Gerda and Idun would want to meet their counterpart.

"I think that can be arranged," he said, "once we get you out of the brig and into some proper quarters."

Chapter Five

BY THE TIME Picard returned to the bridge, Second Officer Wu had arrived as well. The way she looked at the captain told him she had already heard about their unexpected guest, and was as eager as anyone to learn more about her.

Picard smiled to himself. When Wu first came on board the *Stargazer,* her drive and intensity had led to some misunderstandings between her and the rest of the crew. Fortunately, that had changed, and she was now settling in nicely.

"Commander Ben Zoma, Commander Wu, join me in my ready room," the captain said.

Then he entered the room himself, deposited himself in the plastiform chair behind his desk, and called up the file he required. Almost instantly, he found himself looking at a historic set of logs.

"Please," he said without looking up, "have a seat. I will be with you in a moment."

Picard took a moment to read the logs presented to him, refreshing his memory of the events contained in them. As he might have predicted, he had recalled some of the details and forgotten others—including one very important one. Finally, he looked up at his officers.

"Our guest," he said, "claims not to know how she got here. The last thing she remembers is being transported off a ship called *Stargazer.*"

"Really," said Wu.

"And the next thing she knew," Ben Zoma asked, "she was standing there in front of Refsland?"

The captain nodded. "Something like that. It sounds far-fetched, I know. But as she and I we were talking, I recalled something I had learned about at the Academy—an incident in which another apparently simple transport resulted in a bizarre, cross-dimensional transit."

Wu's eyes lit up. "Captain Kirk."

Ben Zoma pointed at Picard. "That's right. The Halkan system, wasn't it?"

The captain nodded. "Sixty-six years ago, Captain James Kirk and his vessel, the *Enterprise,* were engaged in a diplomatic mission to the Halkan system when an ion storm moved into the area. A rather *severe* ion storm.

"Kirk, his chief medical officer, his chief engineer, and his communications officer were to transport down to the Halkans' planet to conduct negotiations for dilithium mining rights. However, the storm interfered with transporter operation and landed the four of them in another universe, while their counterparts from that universe wound up spitting curses from the brig on Kirk's *Enterprise*."

Ben Zoma stroked his chin. "So in that case, there was actually a trade-off—Kirk's people for their counterparts—as if there were some kind of law of conservation of transported matter at work."

"Interesting," said Wu.

"At any rate," Picard continued, "Kirk and his people found themselves in a frame of reference where the Federation was a repressive empire rather than a league of worlds brought together by mutual consent. Impersonating their counterparts, they managed to return to their proper universe, at which time their counterparts were returned as well.

"But before he departed the other universe, Kirk advised the counterpart of Spock, this *Enterprise*'s first officer, that the regime in power couldn't go on. If it didn't mend its barbaric ways, the captain said, it would invite a revolt—the likeliest result being a dark age in which no one would prosper.

"On the other hand," said Picard, "if change came in an orderly fashion, something might be made of the existing power structure. Kirk left it to the Vulcan to effect that change, if he could."

"Unfortunately," Ben Zoma interjected, "Kirk never found out if his advice bore fruit."

"That is correct," said the captain. "He could only guess as to whether the empire of his counterpart survived, and in what form. And we are no better off in that regard than he was."

The three of them pondered the information for a moment. Then Wu spoke up.

"There wasn't any ion storm present when our guest appeared. However, the anomaly was generating a considerable amount of particle turbulence."

"And we haven't been able to identify the depth of the anomaly," said Ben Zoma. "For all we know, it extends into that other universe."

"Or some other," Wu pointed out. "There's mathematical evidence to suggest the existence of an *infinite* number of universes. Lieutenant Asmund could have come from any one of them."

Picard had already embraced that possibility. Otherwise, he would have left the woman in the brig.

The more compelling question, at the moment, was how Lieutenant Asmund had beamed onto the *Stargazer.* Had the anomaly indeed interfered with her transport, sending her from universe to universe instead of from ship to ship?

And was her captain wondering now what had become of her? Without any knowledge of cross-universe transits, was he trying his damnedest to figure out where she might have gone—and how he could get her back?

Perhaps he was. But without help from Picard, the task would almost certainly prove impossible. For that matter, it might prove impossible *with* his help—but he owed it to Lieutenant Asmund and her captain to try.

And he owed it to the Federation as well—in the event that their visitor's arrival here wasn't an accident after all, but something less innocent—regardless of *which* universe she had come from.

"I will ask Mr. Simenon to see if he can find a way to reverse the transport," Picard told his officers. "If anyone can do it, he can."

"Amen," said Ben Zoma.

Acting security chief Pug Joseph had never felt so strange in his life. The woman he was escorting to her quarters looked and sounded so much like the Asmund sisters, he felt he should be able to speak to her the way he spoke to *them*.

Like a friend. Like a person he worked with day in and day out. Like someone he trusted with his life.

But he couldn't. Despite appearances, the woman beside him was a stranger. And until the captain could confirm where she had come from and under what circumstances, Joseph had to treat her with a healthy dose of suspicion.

"Can you tell me something?" she asked as they made their way down the corridor.

"Not if it's anything that could be considered strategic information," Joseph told her.

"It's nothing like that," the woman assured him. "I just wanted to know what the other Asmunds are like."

"Oh," said Joseph. "That."

"I mean, what kind of officers are they? Are they engineers, like me?"

The security chief didn't see any harm in answering. "One is our helm officer. The other is our navigator."

"I see," the woman said, her eyes narrowing as she

considered what he had told her. "Funny. I had an interest in both those areas before I went into engineering."

"Funny," he echoed. But really, no funnier than anything else about her.

"Are they good at what they do?" she asked.

The security chief rolled his eyes. "They're the best. And I'm not just saying that because they're my fellow officers. Any other captain would give his right arm to have Gerda and Idun on his bridge."

The woman looked at him. "Gerda and Idun?"

"Those are their names," he said.

"How interesting. And what do Gerda and Idun do when they're not on duty?"

Joseph smiled. "That's the kind of thing I'd rather *they* told you, if you know what I mean. It's not a security issue or anything. It's just—"

The woman held up her hand. "You don't have to explain, Lieutenant. I understand."

Of course you do, he thought. If *she* couldn't, who *could?*

Ensign Andreas Nikolas was heading for the science section, where he was supposed to help with the sensor scans they were running there on the anomaly.

It wasn't a bad assignment, considering Nikolas was sort of curious about the anomaly, and had already learned the ropes in that section when Lieutenant Valderrama was in charge. His only reservation was the officer in charge now.

He'd heard some strange rumors about Lieutenant Kastiigan—that he had a fascination with death or some such thing. Not being familiar with Kastiigan's species, the ensign didn't know if all Kandilkari were like that or not.

However, he found it unsettling to work under someone who was a little too willing to sacrifice his life. With that kind of attitude, Kastiigan might not be too concerned about the lives of those around him either—and Nikolas was going to be working as closely with the guy as anybody.

Oh well, he thought. At least it would look good in his service file. *"Perished in the line of duty when his superior cranked the neutrino spectrometer too high"* ...

Before he could elaborate on the idea, he came around a bend in the corridor and saw someone approaching him from the other direction. Two someones, actually. Pug Joseph and one of the Asmunds, either Gerda or Idun.

Whichever twin it was, she was wearing a leathery gray tunic, boots of the same color and texture, and formfitting dark-blue pants. And it wasn't just the way she filled out her ensemble that caught Nikolas's eye.

He had never seen either of the Asmunds wearing anything but a uniform or a set of gym togs. *Never.* And as the ensign was pondering that observation, something happened that seemed even more odd to him.

The woman in the gray tunic smiled at him.

No—it was more than a smile. She was positively beaming at him, as if she had never seen anything so pleasing before in her entire life.

But the Asmunds didn't smile at *anyone.* At least, not in *his* experience.

It caught Nikolas completely by surprise—so much

so that he doubted the evidence of his own eyes for a moment. But as he stared back, he saw that he hadn't imagined it.

The woman was *still* smiling at him. At *him.*

Then, before he could say anything, she was gone around another bend in the corridor, along with Mr. Joseph. And Nikolas was left with his mouth hanging open.

Impossible as it seemed, one of the Asmunds had favored him with a smile. But he didn't have the slightest clue which of them it was—Gerda or Idun.

As far as Nikolas was concerned, they looked exactly alike. If there was a way to tell them apart—other than the way they wore their hair, or where they sat when they were on the bridge—he was unaware of it.

But he needed to know which of them he had seen. Because once he knew that, he could find out what that smile had been about.

With that in mind, the ensign bolted after the woman. Unfortunately, he came around the bend too quickly and almost knocked over Lieutenant Ulelo.

Muttering an apology, Nikolas tried to disentangle himself from the com officer. However, it took longer than it should have. And by the time the ensign resumed his pursuit, the object of it had already entered a turbolift.

"Wait!" he blurted.

But it was too late. The doors had already begun sliding together. All Nikolas got was a glimpse of blond hair and blue eyes before the doors closed completely.

Damn, he thought, and hit the heel of his hand against the duranium bulkhead in frustration. Idun—or was it Gerda?—had gotten away.

Then he realized that it didn't matter. All he had to do was catch up with Pug Joseph later and find out which Asmund he had been walking with.

Simple, he told himself. *You'll have your answer before you know it.*

He just didn't know how he would be able to wait.

In Vigo's dream, he was back on Pandril, in a pastel-colored lecture hall with a lofty, arched ceiling and the Three Virtues sculpted in sharp relief on the walls.

Humility was represented by a figure with his eyes downcast and his fists pressed together. Selflessness was offering food from a basket he was carrying. And Stoicism was indifferent to the flame that burned in the cup of his joined palms.

Ejanix was standing in the center of the room, beside a holoprojection of a starship engine's reaction chamber. "Matter," he said, considering the hologram, "and antimatter. What happens when they come together?"

Vigo raised his hand. "They annihilate each other."

"Exactly," said Ejanix, speaking loudly enough for his voice to reverberate majestically from wall to wall. "They annihilate each other—releasing an enormous amount of energy in the process. And it is this energy that propels our starships through the void of space."

The void of space. Vigo loved the phrase. And he especially loved it when it was spoken so passionately.

"Imagine," said Ejanix, "two substances so different

from each other that mere contact between them unleashes that kind of power. How can one hope to control such volatility?"

Vigo had read ahead. He knew that the matter and antimatter that made up starship fuel were stored in magnetic containment vessels until the time came for them to be mixed through the medium of a synthetic dilithium crystal.

Raising his hand again, he offered to share his knowledge—an act of selflessness, and therefore a virtuous act. But at the same time, he felt a certain amount of pride in knowing what others did not, and pride was as much at odds with the virtue of humility as matter was with antimatter.

The virtuous path, Vigo reflected, was not always an easy one to follow.

"Ah," said Ejanix, extending his hand in Vigo's direction, "here's someone who can shed light on the question for us."

The other students turned to look at him. He could feel their scrutiny as if it had weight and substance.

"Tell us, then," Ejanix continued, "how is all this power held at bay?"

Suddenly, Vigo noticed that his instructor's hand wasn't empty. It held a phaser—a type that Vigo had never seen before—and it was trained directly at Vigo's forehead.

"Get up," Ejanix told him.

Vigo didn't understand. "What do you mean?" he asked.

"Get up," his instructor said again.

But this time his voice was considerably deeper, considerably harsher. Much more so, in fact, than Vigo would ever have imagined possible.

He was about to ask if there was something wrong with his instructor's throat when something happened— something shockingly and devastatingly painful.

Vigo cried out—or thought he did—and found himself on a carpeted surface in a dimly lit room. There was a twisted length of blanket on the floor beside him, one corner of which was wrapped around his thigh. Other than that, he was dressed in just his sleeping pants.

And his jaw hurt. It hurt *terribly*—as if someone had struck it with a hunk of metal as hard as he could.

That's when Vigo realized that he wasn't in a lecture hall after all. He wasn't even on Pandril. He was in the modest quarters assigned to him at the development facility on Wayland Prime.

Nor did he have to look far to explain why his jaw hurt, or how he had fallen out of bed. The explanation was hovering over him in the form of a figure too big and blue and hairless to be anything but another Pandrilite.

But it wasn't Ejanix, the weapons officer noted. It was someone else, dressed in civilian clothing and armed with a phaser pistol, which—as in Vigo's dream—was pointed right at his forehead.

It didn't make sense, he insisted inwardly. This was a secure Starfleet installation. There shouldn't have been any civilians in it, armed or otherwise.

And yet...

Vigo peered at the intruder as he got to his feet. "Who are you?" he asked. "What do you want?"

The fellow didn't answer either question. He just used his phaser to gesture toward the door, momentarily removing Vigo from its line of fire.

It was as big a window of opportunity as the weapons officer could reasonably have expected—which was to say it wasn't big at all. But if he were lucky, it would be all he needed.

Without hesitation, he launched himself in the other Pandrilite's direction, his right hand reaching for the phaser while his left grabbed for the fellow's throat.

The intruder cried out and pressed the trigger on his weapon, but by then Vigo had thrust it off line. The seething, red beam shot past his ear and struck the bulkhead behind him.

Vigo heard the wail of tortured metal, but he didn't have time to examine the damage. He was too busy using his grasp on his assailant's throat to smash the fellow's head against the wall behind him.

Flesh and bone struck the duranium surface with an audible thud, an indication of the considerable force behind the blow. But the intruder was a Pandrilite. It would take more than that to knock him out.

A second time, Vigo slammed his adversary's head into the wall. And a third. Then he switched gears, pivoted into the intruder and wrenched at the phaser as hard as he could.

As he had hoped, it came free in his hands. But his adversary hadn't quite had all the fight knocked out of him. No sooner had Vigo gotten sole possession of the weapon than he felt a fist bludgeon the back of his neck.

Fireworks went off in the weapons officer's brain, but he

didn't dare falter. Driving his elbow into the other Pan-drilite's ribs, he sent him staggering backward. Then he whirled and lashed out with his foot at his adversary's chin.

The impact snapped the intruder's head back and sent him flying into the wall. Immediately, Vigo turned the setting on the phaser to stun—but as it turned out, he didn't have to use it. His assailant slid to the floor and lay there at an awkward angle, unmoving.

Finally, Vigo had a chance to get his bearings. *Think,* he told himself, as he drew in a deep, welcome breath. *If there's one intruder, there may be more.*

Just as the thought crossed his mind, he heard the rasp of voices out in the corridor. They were coming from off to Vigo's right, where Sebring and Runj had their quarters.

At least one of the voices was deep and resonant enough to belong to a Pandrilite. And it was giving or-ders, the same way Vigo's assailant had done.

Another voice sounded like it was protesting. The more Vigo listened, the more it sounded like Runj. No one else at the installation was likely to be slurring his words so badly.

Like Vigo, it seemed, the Vobilite had been assaulted in his sleep. Maybe Sebring as well.

But it took a security override to get into someone's quarters—or else an intimate knowledge of the door-locking mechanism. How could the intruders have got-ten either one of those things?

And where were the installation's security officers? Why hadn't they detected the intruders' arrival in time to lock the place down?

Vigo forced himself to put such questions aside for

the moment, knowing he had more immediate concerns. The voices in the corridor were getting closer by the second.

"Antazi!" one of them called.

It was a Pandrilite name—probably that of the fellow who had woken Vigo up. Apparently, his compatriots wanted to know if he was all right.

Vigo answered—in his own way. Swinging out into the corridor with his phaser at the ready, he fired at the first unfamiliar face he could find—another Pandrilite, as it turned out. The beam catapulted Antazi's friend into the air and dropped him on the deck, unconscious.

But there was another big, blue figure right behind him, a phaser in one hand and Sebring's arm in the other. Seeing his comrade go down, he extended his weapon in Vigo's direction—but as he fired, the human lowered his shoulder and spoiled his captor's aim.

It was all the opening Vigo needed. His phaser beam speared the intruder and sent him skidding down the corridor, bereft of his senses.

"Nice shot," said Sebring, disarming the Pandrilite who had woken him. He had a nasty-looking cut over one eye. "These guys friends of yours?"

Vigo knew that the human was only half-serious. Still, he said, "I've never seen them before in my life."

But they *were* all Pandrilites. He found that curious, considering his people seldom ventured offworld, much less hired themselves out as mercenaries.

Runj joined them, a phaser in his hand now too. "Any idea what they're after?"

Vigo shook his head. "Not specifically, no. But in a place like this, it could be a great many things."

Sebring looked up and down the corridor. "You can say that again, pal. I just wish I knew how many of these slime devils we're up against."

"We could go through the installation one hallway at a time," Runj said around his tusks, "and find out that way. But I wouldn't advise it. I think we can be reasonably certain that they outnumber us."

"Also," said Vigo, "they may have taken hostages. That will make it a good deal more difficult for us to fight them."

Sebring swore beneath his breath. "And if the research our people have been doing here falls into the wrong hands..." His voice trailed off, leaving the rest to their imagination.

Vigo nodded. The research had to be their priority. But there were only three of them. How could they win against a potentially much larger force?

Then it came to him. "The intruders couldn't have beamed down—not with that magnetic-storm belt out there. They had to descend in a shuttle, just as we did."

Runj looked at him. "And they'll need to take that shuttle back up."

"Exactly," said Vigo.

"So if we disable the thing," Sebring reasoned, "they can't leave with it."

"Or what they came for," Runj added. "At least until they can send down another shuttle."

"If they even have one," said Vigo.

Sebring shrugged. "Sounds like a plan to me."

"But we've got to strike now," said Runj, "before they realize we're on the loose."

Vigo agreed wholeheartedly. "Let's go," he said, as he made his way to the nearest exit past the motionless bodies of his fellow Pandrilites.

Chapter Six

GREYHORSE WAS RECALIBRATING the sensor array on one of his biobeds when, out of the corner of his eye, he caught sight of two people entering sickbay.

One of them, he knew, was Pug Joseph. The other was the individual who had beamed aboard the ship recently under mysterious circumstances.

Taking a deep breath, Greyhorse gathered himself. Then, slowly and deliberately, he looked up.

And saw her.

The doctor had been warned by the captain as to what was coming his way. But he hadn't been warned strongly enough or thoroughly enough to prepare him for the sight that greeted his eyes.

He had expected to see someone who looked like his lover but wasn't, someone along the lines of Gerda's sister Idun. But the woman who had just walked into Greyhorse's sickbay *was* Gerda. At least, it seemed that way. And yet, in a profoundly disturbing way, she *wasn't.*

The doctor couldn't explain why he felt that way about her. And yet, he did.

The woman smiled as she and Joseph approached him—and that too was shocking in its way, because Gerda had never smiled that way, nor would she. But the newcomer was smiling in the very way Greyhorse was certain Gerda would have smiled if she had ever been inclined to do so.

"Doctor Greyhorse?" the woman ventured.

He cleared his throat to buy himself some time. "Yes," he said at last, with an annoying quaver in his voice. "That's correct. I'm Doctor Greyhorse."

"Best doctor in the quadrant," Joseph chipped in. "Don't worry, Lieutenant. You're in good hands."

"I'm sure I am," said the newcomer.

Greyhorse ignored both their compliments. "Though you seem to have suffered no ill effects," he said, "the captain felt it was only prudent for me to look you over."

"Of course," the woman said. She looked around. "Where would you like me to sit?"

Greyhorse indicated another biobed with a gesture. "This will do. You have biobeds in your universe, don't you?"

"We do," the woman confirmed as she moved to the device and slid onto its surface. "But I don't think they're quite as advanced as the ones you have." She shrugged in a way the doctor found immensely appealing. "Not that I'm an expert on such things."

Greyhorse decided that it would be best to minimize

his conversation with the newcomer and avoid her gaze. He found it too confusing to do otherwise.

"This won't take long," he assured her in his most clinical voice. Then he punched the requisite studs in the side of the bed and examined his readouts.

His patient was human right down to the cellular level. The captain would be pleased to learn that, at least.

She was healthy as well. If she had suffered any ill effects as a result of her transit from universe to universe, they didn't show up on his scans.

No evidence of exposure to any of the more exotic diseases either—just as the transporter's biofilter had indicated. Not even Hesperan thumping cough, which most of the crew had contracted at one time or another.

Greyhorse checked for signs of plastic surgery, but couldn't find any. Her hair, eye, and skin color were natural. And when he compared her genetic makeup with his file data on Gerda and Idun, he found that she matched them almost exactly.

All in all, the newcomer was just what she seemed— an exact duplicate of Gerda and Idun Asmund, every bit as close to them as they were to each other.

"Do I pass?" she asked.

He couldn't help glancing at her. She was smiling again. But then, she had never been raised by Klingons or exposed to the savagery of their culture. She had grown up in some other, more human—more *civilized*— milieu, and it showed.

"You do," he said flatly, doing his best to conceal all of the emotions he was feeling.

The strongest of them, surprisingly, was fear. Greyhorse was very much afraid that he would find this pleasant, easygoing, undeniably more *human* version of his lover more attractive than Gerda herself.

"We're done?" asked Joseph.

The doctor turned to him. "You are. I'll contact the captain with my findings." Then he glanced at his patient again; it was unavoidable. "Thank you for your time."

"Don't mention it," she told him.

Then she lowered herself off the biobed and glanced at Joseph. "Shall we?"

The acting security chief didn't say anything. He just smiled and nodded. Then he accompanied the woman as she made her way to the exit.

Greyhorse found himself envying Joseph. He wanted the newcomer to stay so he could get to know her better. He wanted to find out in what ways she differed from Gerda—and in what ways she was the same.

However, he didn't ask her to come back. He retreated to his office instead.

It was only when he was safely inside the enclosure that he slumped into his chair, let his head fall back, and breathed a heartfelt sigh of relief.

Vigo stopped and waited for his Starfleet colleagues to catch up with him.

To this point, luck had been on their side. They had made their way through half the installation without running into any of the intruders, Pandrilite or otherwise.

Now they were standing just inside the arch of an exit door—the same door from which Riyyen had emerged to welcome Vigo on his arrival. *So far so good,* he thought. But their next step would be a tougher one.

Vigo looked at Sebring and then at Runj. "It's a cloudy night," he said, recalling the meteorological scan he had seen before he went to sleep. "We'll have that going for us."

"Great," said Sebring, in a sarcastic tone. "What could possibly go wrong?"

The Pandrilite resisted the urge to answer him. Without another word, he pressed the metal plate next to the door. It opened as if there were nothing amiss—no security breach, no invaders, and no possibility of the Federation losing some of its best-kept secrets.

As Vigo had expected, the sky was blanketed with clouds. The planet's moon was on the other side of them, leaving the terrain outside the installation all but lightless.

Fortunately, they didn't need much light to find their target—a craft that looked a lot like the cargo vehicles in the *Stargazer*'s shuttlebay, no doubt outfitted to hold people instead. It sat out there in the middle of the landing area, which lay between the extremities of the horseshoe-shaped building and had played host to perhaps hundreds of shuttle landings since the installation was built.

But all those other shuttles had carried Starfleet personnel, equipment, or supplies. This one had carried down a squadron of armed invaders. And to Vigo's chagrin, at least one of them was standing guard over it now.

"Damn," said Sebring. "There's someone there."

"So it would seem," said Runj, his lip curling in disgust over his tusks.

The figure was on the other side of the shuttle, and he

appeared to be gazing in another direction. But he would notice them soon enough if they tried to approach him.

Sebring's eyes narrowed appraisingly. "I bet we could take him out with one shot."

"But what if there's someone inside the shuttle?" Runj asked. "He would take off before we could get to him."

"And contact his comrades in the installation," Vigo added. "We wouldn't stand a chance."

"So we need to get close to the thing before we make our move," Sebring observed. "The question is...how?"

Vigo considered the problem for a moment—which was about all the time they could spare, considering the intruders might find out they were on the loose at any moment.

"One of us will have to distract and incapacitate the guard," he decided, "while the other two circle around behind him and go after the shuttle."

Neither of his colleagues argued with the plan. But then, they were rather limited in their options.

There was only one decision left to be made. "Who will be the decoy?" asked Runj.

Vigo eyed the guard. "I will."

Sebring looked at him. "You sure?"

Vigo nodded. "From what we've seen, all the invaders are Pandrilites. I may be able to confuse him for a moment, make him think I'm one of them."

His colleagues seemed to accept that. It would be dangerous for Vigo, no question about it. But then, it would be dangerous for all of them.

"All right," said Sebring. He exchanged glances with the Vobilite, and then with Vigo. "Let's go get him."

Without hesitation, Sebring moved off to the left over the short, wiry turf, while Runj worked his way to the right. They moved quickly and quietly, looking like shadows on the walls.

Vigo waited until he thought his fellow officers had placed themselves in position. Then he took a deep breath and moved out from concealment.

"Help…" he groaned, grabbing his belly as if he'd been hit there. He staggered forward. "Help me…."

The guard turned around and looked past the shuttle, tilting his head in an effort to see better. "Who is it? What happened?"

"They're right behind me…" Vigo gasped, doubling over as he advanced so the Pandrilite couldn't see his face. "We've got to get out of here…before it's too late…."

The guard just stood there, caught between concern and caution. "Suddig?" he ventured, mistaking the weapons officer for one of the other invaders.

"Yes," Vigo grated as he lumbered forward, carrying his deception as far as he could. "Help me, please…."

Finally putting his wariness aside, the guard rushed across the intervening space, his weapon in hand. "Don't worry, I've got you," he assured his fellow Pandrilite.

No, thought Vigo. I've *got* you.

As soon as the guard was within a few meters of him, he leaned forward just a little more and gradually accelerated his stagger into a headlong rush. Before the guard knew what was happening, Vigo was bearing him to the ground.

The guard uttered a strangled cry and squeezed a shot off, but it missed the weapons officer and struck the ground instead, leaving a long, black streak of smoking turf.

Vigo had the upper hand, but the guard wasn't easy to knock out. After all, he was a Pandrilite. Vigo had to drive his fist into the intruder's face once, twice, and a third time before he finally went limp.

That done, the weapons officer stripped his adversary of his weapons—both the one in his hand and another that Vigo found in his belt. Then he slung the intruder over his shoulder and lumbered the rest of the way to the shuttle.

Sebring and Runj were there already. They signaled to him that the vehicle was empty. On the other hand, they didn't have any easy way to get inside it.

And they couldn't simply fire into the plasma exhaust. Not unless they wanted to blow themselves up, and half the installation into the bargain.

"We need to get to the controls," Vigo said as he came around the shuttle and dumped the intruder on the ground.

"That means getting inside," the Vobilite noted.

"No problem," said Sebring, hunkering down and resetting his borrowed weapon. "I haven't yet met the shuttle hull that can stand up to a good dose of phaser fire."

Fortunately, Sebring and Runj were able to use the craft for cover while they worked. But Vigo remained standing, so a casual observer might think the guard was still out there.

As Vigo watched, his colleagues unleashed a seething red barrage at the center of the hatch door. Little by little, the door's duranium skin blackened and rippled.

Suddenly, the Pandrilite heard shouting from across the landing area. Looking back over his shoulder, he saw a trio of angry Pandrilites running toward them.

Sebring and Runj heard them too. But the weapons officers didn't give any thought to defending themselves. They left that to Vigo and kept working on the hatch door—even when a couple of phaser beams sizzled past the shuttle, missing it by inches on either side.

No longer compelled to impersonate the unconscious guard, Vigo fired back. One of his phaser bursts found an intruder and sent him sprawling, but that only made the other two fan out to make it harder for him.

And a moment later, two more of them came out of the installation, their phasers blazing. The weapons officers were caught in a swiftly developing crossfire, beams of directed energy stabbing the night like fiery needles.

"Come on," growled Sebring, his face crimson with reflected phaser light as he and Runj dug their way into the shuttle. "Just a little more."

Vigo managed to pick off the intruder on his right flank, but it gave the one on his left a clear shot at Runj and Sebring. The *Stargazer* officer moved around the Vobilite to screen him, to buy him a little more time.

But he was a fraction of a second too late. One of the enemy's beams slammed into Runj and laid him out flat.

Vigo returned the intruder's fire but missed, his energy burst vanishing into the darkness beyond the landing field. And before he could take aim again, a beam from another direction nearly took his head off.

"There!" said Sebring, his voice full of triumph. Indeed, Vigo could see through a charred, blistered hole into the shuttle's interior. "We're through! Now if I can just—"

But before the human could finish, he was bludgeoned by a bloodred beam. As he fell forward against the shuttle, Vigo fired back. Then he turned and peered through the opening his colleagues had made.

It was big enough, he estimated, for him to slip his hand through and reach the instrument panel. Runj and Sebring might not have been able to do it, but *he* could.

Squeezing off another blast at the enemy to his left, Vigo sent him scurrying and secured a moment's respite. He used it to peek inside and get a look at the craft's controls.

As he had expected, they weren't any different from what one might have seen in a *Stargazer* shuttle. And if that were so, he knew exactly what to do.

By that time, the intruder on his left was taking aim at him. Fortunately, Vigo was quicker. He nailed the Pandrilite square in the chest.

But he didn't watch the intruder go flying backward into the darkness. He was too busy thrusting his left arm into the hole in the shuttle's hull.

It went in up to his shoulder before his fingers touched the control panel. By feel alone, he groped his way to what he hoped was the right set of studs. Then he began pressing them in just the right order.

At the same time, another intruder moved into view past the edge of the shuttle. With the phaser in his right hand, the weapons officer sent a crimson beam slicing through the night—while with his left hand, he continued his manipulation of the control panel.

Another second, he thought. *Just another second…*

A blast of phaser fire glanced off the skin of the shuttle, blinding him. But it didn't keep him from doing his touchwork on the panel.

Almost done, Vigo told himself, firing barrages to one side and then the other even though he couldn't quite see what he was firing at.

Finally, he touched the last stud in the sequence—and heard the shuttle's systems spiral down into a well of silence. Only the craft's life supports, which drew on a backup battery, continued to function.

Another beam struck the shuttle and glanced off it, missing his head by a handsbreadth or less. But he didn't let it faze him. Pulling his arm back out of the hole, he replaced it with the barrel of his weapon.

Then Vigo pressed the trigger—and saw the control panel erupt in a spurt of white-hot sparks. That was important if he was to cover up his handiwork. Just to be certain, he kept firing at the thing, watching the sparks start to spawn tongues of pale blue flame.

Keep going, he thought. *As long as you—*

But before he could get any further, he felt something hit him with bone-shattering force. It drove the breath from his lungs and the feeling from his body, leaving him quaking and all but inert.

He tried to continue firing into the shuttle, but to no avail. As if from a distance, he saw the phaser fall from his hand and hit the ground.

Come on, he urged himself. *Pick it up.*

But as he bent to retrieve the weapon, he felt another impact. And a moment later, he slipped into darkness.

Chapter Seven

WHEN NIKOLAS ENTERED the ship's mess hall, he could barely contain his impatience—or his excitement.

He wanted to share it, too. So when he saw his friend Obal, he headed right for him. He didn't even stop to get a tray full of food from the replicator.

"You look cheerful," Obal observed as Nikolas sat down opposite him.

"That," said the ensign, "is because the most amazing thing just happened to me."

"Oh?" said the Binderian.

"It was unbelievable," said Nikolas. "I was walking down the corridor and I saw one of the Asmunds coming the other way with Lieutenant Joseph." He shook his head, still unable to believe it. "And she smiled at me."

The security officer looked understandably perplexed. "How unusual…" he remarked.

Nikolas laughed. "You're not kidding it's unusual. I mean, it wasn't just one of those 'have a nice day' smiles. I'm telling you, her whole face lit up. It looked like she was really happy to see me."

"Remarkable," said Obal. "But—"

"Now," said Nikolas, "all I have to do is figure out whether it was Gerda or Idun and take it from there."

"Actually," said the Binderian, his brow puckering, "it may be neither of them."

The ensign looked at him. "What are you talking about?"

"You obviously haven't heard, but there is a third Asmund aboard at the moment."

Nikolas studied his friend's face, which was as serious as he had ever seen it. "You're joking, right?"

"I'm afraid I'm not," said the security officer. "The woman who smiled at you...what was she wearing? Was it a Starfleet uniform or something else?"

"Something else," Nikolas recalled.

"The black togs the Asmunds often wear when they work out?"

Nikolas shook his head. "No. Gray tunic. Gray boots. And dark blue pants."

Obal nodded judiciously. "Then the woman you saw was neither Gerda nor Idun, but the third Asmund of whom I spoke."

Nikolas didn't get it. "What are you saying? That they're triplets all of a sudden?"

"What I am saying," Obal told him, "is that the Asmunds seem to have a counterpart in another universe, and she arrived on the *Stargazer* a bit more than an hour ago."

Nikolas frowned. Obviously, he had missed something while he was down in the science section. "Maybe you'd better start at the beginning, pal. And go nice and slow, all right?"

Obal agreed that he would do that.

Gerda frowned and shifted her weight in her seat. This was taking a very long time. At least, it seemed that way.

"What's keeping them?" she asked her sister.

They were sitting on two of the three chairs in Idun's anteroom—a couple of Klingon chairs fashioned from wrought iron. The third chair, which was made of softer materials to accommodate non-Klingon guests, was conspicuous by its emptiness.

Idun shrugged. "Pug only called about a minute ago. Maybe it is turbolift traffic."

It was a jest—Gerda knew that. But she was too jittery to chuckle at it. "Do you think they stopped somewhere along the way?" she asked.

"It is possible," Idun allowed. "But—"

A chime interrupted her, signaling that someone was waiting in the corridor outside the door.

Idun glanced at her sister. "Enter."

A moment later, Pug Joseph walked in. And right behind him was a woman who looked exactly like Gerda and Idun, down to the last feature and detail.

Even her hair was cut like the twins'. The only aspect of her appearance that set her apart was her clothing, which was of a decidedly civilian variety.

Gerda found herself staring at the newcomer. And the

newcomer was staring right back, turning from Gerda to Idun and back again.

"It's hard to believe what I'm looking at," the woman said, in a voice that could have been Gerda's or Idun's. "Not just one of me, but *two*."

Idun nodded. "It's strange, all right."

"I'll be right outside," Pug said. "You three sound like you've got a lot to talk about."

Gerda nodded, acknowledging the gesture. As soon as the security officer was outside, the door slid closed behind him—leaving the three of them alone.

The newcomer smiled a little awkwardly. "Well, this is something you don't see every day."

Idun laughed a short Klingon laugh. "I suppose not." She tilted her head as if to get a better look at their guest. "We're told that you're from another universe."

"That's the theory," the woman said. "And I certainly haven't got a better explanation."

"If that's so," said Gerda, "you must be one of us— my sister or myself. The question is which one."

The newcomer shook her head. "I'm not certain. You see, I'm a twin as well." A shadow seemed to fall over her expression. "Or rather, I was."

Gerda felt a chill. "What happened?"

"An unforeseen complication at birth. The doctors did what they could, it seems, but to no avail. My sister died."

Gerda exchanged uncomfortable glances with Idun. It was eerie to think that if they had been born in that other universe instead of their own, one of them might not have survived.

"Unfortunate," Idun observed solemnly.

Their guest nodded. "I've always thought so."

"What was your sister's name?" Gerda asked, hoping the reply would give them a roundabout answer to her question.

The response was a wistful one. "Her name was Helga."

Gerda concealed her disappointment. If the name of the twin who had died was different from both hers and her sister's, the one who had lived and sat before them now might be named neither Gerda nor Idun.

Her name might be Ailsa. Or Freyja. Or Dana, or a host of other possibilities.

In that case, they would probably never determine whose counterpart she was. Gerda began to see why the woman hadn't simply answered their question directly.

Idun had likely come to the same conclusion. However, she took the next step anyway. "So what *is* your name?"

The newcomer shrugged. "Gerda Idun."

Idun smiled at the twist of fate. "So...you were given *both* our names?"

"Yes," said Gerda Idun. "It's a long story, I'm afraid."

"We have time," Gerda assured her.

The newcomer sighed. "Orginally, my parents intended to name one of us Gerda and the other Idun— just as yours did. But my sister left us before my parents could decide who was to be who. And since my mother didn't want to horrify either of her aunts by giving her name to the baby who had died..."

Idun nodded. "She named her Helga."

"Exactly as our mother would have done," said

Gerda. "She was always afraid of what her aunts would say as well."

"Then you understand," said Gerda Idun, obviously pleased that it was so. "Not everyone does, you know."

"Not everyone is *you*," said Idun.

They all sat in silence for a moment, appreciating the bizarre irony of the remark. But it wasn't an especially uncomfortable silence—no more so than sitting with oneself.

"Are your parents still alive?" Gerda asked at last.

Gerda Idun shook her head. "They passed away a few years ago, within a couple of months of each other. From Belliard's bipolar disease."

Not a good way to go, Gerda thought. "I hope they weren't in too much pain."

"Not *too* much," said Gerda Idun. But the noticeable tremor in her voice made it clear that she was understating the truth. "And your parents?"

"Killed also," said Idun, "but not by disease. They were private cargo haulers—engine components, EPS couplings, that sort of thing."

"Their routes carried them well beyond the boundaries of Federation space," Gerda noted. "They routinely ran into Orions, Athaban, Talarians."

"It sounds like dangerous work," said Gerda Idun.

"It was," Idun confirmed. "A bit too dangerous for most other cargo haulers. But our parents were excellent pilots, and they never tried to take on more than they could handle." She glanced at Gerda. "Until one day, they ran into a squadron of Pephili raiders."

"It was a one-in-a-million encounter," said Gerda, recalling the stricken looks on her parents' faces when they realized what they were up against. "The kind of thing that's not supposed to happen out in space. We came out of a nebula and there they were, no doubt every bit as surprised as we were."

Idun heaved a sigh. "Once the Pephili had our ship in their sights, they weren't going to stop until they stripped us of our cargo—and our lives. Our father led them on a chase, but he couldn't elude them forever. Finally, they hit one of our warp nacelles. Our parents knew it was only a matter of time before the cowards caught up with us, so they looked for a planet on which to set down."

The memory was like ashes in Gerda's mouth. "We found a class-M world and landed safely in the midst of some hills. But the Pephili came after us with a party of armed thugs." She felt a lump in her throat and willed it away, knowing it wasn't worthy of her. "They killed our parents, stole our cargo, and took whatever else they could rip from our ship. Then they left us there to die."

Gerda Idun looked from one of the sisters to the other. "Just the two of you?"

Idun nodded. "Just the two of us. We were eight years old. And the land around us was barren as far as the eye could see. For several days, we lived on scraps we found in our ship's pantry. Then we ran out of even those. We fully expected to starve to death, but we didn't have the courage to set out across the wastes and try to do something about it. So we sat and waited quietly for death."

"Then," said Gerda, "a ship appeared." She could see it in her mind's eye—a dark speck against a pale orange sky, growing bigger with each passing moment. "It was a *Klingon* scout ship, but we didn't know that. We thought it might be the Pephili, coming back to kill us as they had killed our parents. So we ran into the hills and hid."

"Still," said Idun, "they found us—a squad of Klingon warriors, surprised to find a strange ship on a world they had long ago made part of their empire. We had never seen Klingons before, so we didn't know what to expect of them. But they took us back to their ship and presented us to their captain, a warrior named Warrokh."

"He seemed to like something about us," said Gerda, "though I can't imagine what it was. We were pathetic—cringing, mewling little girls, too frightened to even look him in the eye. As it happened, he and his wife Chithar were childless. Warrokh thought it would please her to take us in and make us their own."

Idun nodded, her eyes glazed with memory. "And that is what they did."

Gerda Idun looked at them, her expression one of disbelief. "These Klingons...adopted you?"

Gerda nodded. "They took us into their House and made us their legal heirs, according us rights and privileges as if we were their own blood."

The newcomer winced. "But Klingon society is so...different from ours. It must have been..." She seemed to search for a word.

"Rigorous? Painful? Terrifying?" Idun suggested. "It was all of that—and more."

"And we were still mourning our parents," Gerda noted, "wrestling with the feelings any newly orphaned human child would have felt."

Gerda Idun's brow puckered. "You say 'human' as if you've become something else."

"We *have*," Gerda told her. "We've become Klingons."

"Not literally, of course," said Idun. "But in all the ways that matter—and there are many of them."

Gerda Idun seemed to consider the remark. Finally, she said, "How different our lives have been."

"Have you had any contact with Klingons?" asked Gerda.

The newcomer shook her head. "Where I come from, Klingons are our enemies—the enemies of *humans,* that is."

Idun grunted. "That was once true of our universe as well. It was only about forty years ago, at the historic Khitomer Conference, that the situation began to change."

"Now," said Gerda, "the Federation and the Empire are no longer enemies."

"Though," Idun added, "I sometimes think there are those in the Empire who would have it otherwise."

Gerda Idun laughed. And though Idun wasn't normally given to laughter, she laughed along with her.

Gerda saw something in the newcomer's eyes then— something that appeared and then disappeared with the speed of a stray thought. It was so quick, so fleeting, that she had to wonder if it had happened at all.

"Well," said Gerda Idun, "it was nice talking with you, but I really ought to get some sleep. With all that's happened, I've been up for about twenty hours now."

"We understand," said Idun.

"Besides," the newcomer added with a sly little

smirk, "I don't want your captain to think we're in here plotting to take over the ship."

Idun chuckled. And she wasn't the chuckling sort—not any more than Gerda was.

The navigator watched for that look in Gerda Idun's eyes, but she didn't see it this time. Even more so than before, she had to wonder if it had merely been a figment of her imagination.

"I hope we'll be able to do this again," said Gerda Idun. Then she got up and headed for the door.

"Wait," said Idun, getting to her feet as well.

Gerda Idun stopped and looked back at her. "Yes?"

"You'll need a change of clothes," said the helm officer.

Their guest dismissed the idea with a gesture. "I can get a set from the replicator."

"You can," Idun agreed. "But why waste the energy it takes to replicate new garments when we can lend you some of *ours?*" She turned to her sister. "What do you think?"

Gerda thought it made sense. Waste was a sin, or so she had been brought up to believe. "We have more than we need."

Gerda Idun looked grateful. "All right. If that's the way you feel. Thanks—both of you."

Idun inclined her head. "Thanks are unnecessary."

"You would do the same for us," Gerda said—and found herself watching their counterpart's reaction.

The woman nodded. "I would like to think so."

Then she really did leave. As the door to Idun's quarters whispered closed behind Gerda Idun, Gerda's sister turned to her with an expression of approval on her face.

"Remarkable," she said.

Gerda nodded. "Indeed."

But she wasn't sure that she approved of Gerda Idun as much as her sister did.

Chapter Eight

VIGO WOKE TO FIND a face looming in front of him. A Pandrilite face. A very *angry* Pandrilite face, with a scar running down the side of it.

"What did you do to the shuttle?" the Pandrilite demanded.

Vigo was sitting in a chair with his hands tied behind him, a massive headache throbbing behind his eyes. His ribs hurt too, as if someone had punched him repeatedly. But then, he reflected, phasers were *designed* to do damage.

"I asked you a question," said his interrogator.

Vigo remained silent. If the fellow wanted help with his shuttle repairs, he would have to find it elsewhere.

The intruder stepped back, giving the weapons officer a better view of his surroundings. He was in the installation's mess hall. Neither Sebring nor Runj nor any of the installation's Starfleet personnel was in sight, but there were six or seven Pandrilites in evidence.

To Vigo's consternation, Ejanix was one of them. It angered the weapons officer to think that these marauders could hurt his friend and there wouldn't be anything he could do about it.

Then he caught Ejanix's eyes and saw that his mentor didn't share his concern. He looked annoyed, even a little fidgety, but hardly in fear for his life.

Vigo didn't understand. As he was trying to puzzle it out, his interrogator leaned closer again.

"It's only a matter of time before you tell me," he insisted. "Why not save us all some trouble?"

Vigo averted his eyes.

When he sabotaged the shuttle, he had wondered if the intruders had another one at their disposal. Judging by the intensity with which he was being questioned, he guessed that they didn't.

So until they could fix *this* one, they were trapped here.

The muscles in the intruder's jaw rippled. Then he smiled, though his eyes remained hard with restrained anger.

"We have an interesting situation here," he said. "There are three of you I can question—three of you who sabotaged the shuttle. However, I only need an answer from one of you, which makes the other two expendable."

That got Vigo's attention. Still, he kept his eyes turned away from the intruder.

"Maybe you don't think I'm determined to get an answer," said the fellow with the scar. "Maybe you require a demonstration. Or maybe you would like to *be* the demonstration."

Vigo remained silent.

His interrogator grabbed his face suddenly, as if he had every intention of tearing it off. His fingers were strong, viselike, even by Pandrilite standards.

"I'm warning you," he said, his voice low and dangerous.

But Vigo didn't talk. Nor would he.

The intruder studied him for a moment, his eyes full of cold fury. Then he let go of Vigo's face, took a step back, and said, "Kill him."

"No!" Ejanix blurted, stepping in front of Vigo as the intruder's men raised their weapons. He looked horror-stricken. "What in the name of the Virtues are you doing?"

The scarred man didn't take his eyes off Vigo. "Eliminating a nuisance," he responded evenly.

"You promised me no one would die," Ejanix protested. "You said that, Kovajo."

The intruder's men looked to him. He considered Vigo a moment longer, his lip curling as if in disgust. Then he gestured for his subordinates to lower their weapons.

Kovajo turned to Ejanix. "I'm sorry," he said, though he didn't sound especially remorseful. "You're right. When we discussed the ways in which you could help us seize this installation, I said no one would die."

Suddenly, his fist was hurtling at Vigo. The weapons officer barely had time to turn his face to avoid the impact. Still, the blow was a heavy one. It dazed him, sent the chair he was in crashing to the floor.

A moment later, he felt himself being picked up. The

front legs of his chair hit the floor again, and he again found himself facing the man Ejanix had called Kovajo.

Vigo tasted blood as he braced himself for another blow. But it didn't come. At least, not right away.

"On the other hand," said Kovajo, his voice marked by an eerie calm, "I didn't promise that no one would be punished." His left eye twitched as if with barely restrained fury. "And punished they will be."

"There's no need," Ejanix insisted. "They're your prisoners already. They can't hurt you."

"Maybe it's not for what they're going to do," said Kovajo. "Maybe it's for what they've already done."

"I did it by myself," Vigo insisted through the thickening bruise on one side of his mouth. "The others had nothing to do with it."

That elicited a smile from Kovajo. "How noble," he said. "You have a lot to learn." He glanced at one of the Pandrilites behind him. "Take him away."

Vigo turned to his mentor. Ejanix looked torn, conflicted. But he didn't say anything more as Kovajo's men untied Vigo and pushed him out the door.

As Gerda always did when she sat down at her navigation console, she checked all her monitors for problems. Then she ran a quick diagnostic to make sure all her instruments were working as they should have been.

Since there were neither problems nor malfunctions, she turned to her sister. Idun was finishing her own set of diagnostics at the helm controls—her face caught in the glare of the bridge's forward viewscreen, where the anomaly was glowing with dark purple fury.

They hadn't discussed Gerda Idun since their meeting in Idun's quarters. However, Gerda had been thinking about their counterpart a great deal.

In the course of her reflection, she had come to believe that it wasn't her imagination after all. She had seen something in Gerda Idun's expression that was at odds with the persona she presented—something that made Gerda mistrust her, despite the woman's resemblance to her.

And yet, Idun appeared not to have noticed anything. Or if she had, she hadn't said anything about it—a situation the navigator meant to investigate in short order.

"It was interesting," she said, "how different our counterpart was from either one of us. Without a Klingon upbringing to nurture her better qualities, she might as well have been any human."

Idun looked at her as if she had brought a pet *targ* onto the bridge. "I'm a little surprised to hear you say that. I thought she was a lot like *you.*"

"Like *me?*" Gerda asked. It was about the last thing she had expected to hear. "She's *nothing* like me."

"Isn't she?" Idun asked. She shrugged.

"Nothing at all," Gerda insisted, unable to see how her sister had come to such a conclusion.

Idun turned back to her instruments and fell silent for a moment. However, her expression indicated that she hadn't wavered in her opinion.

"In any case," the helm officer said finally, "we need to take Gerda Idun under our wing. Being from another universe, she must feel quite lost here."

"No doubt," said Gerda.

But she didn't feel the same sense of responsibility

that her sister did. Obviously, Idun had indeed missed what Gerda spotted in the newcomer's expression, or she wouldn't have been speaking of her this way.

But I saw something, Gerda insisted silently. *I did. I'm certain of it.*

"After all," Idun continued, "our blood runs in her veins. That makes her family."

Gerda didn't look at it that way. Members of the same house didn't keep things from each other, and it seemed to her that Gerda Idun was doing just that. But without the least shred of proof to support her suspicions, the navigator wasn't ready to oppose her sister's point of view.

"We will do what we can," she said.

Then she turned back to the viewscreen, where the anomaly glared at her like a great, blazing eye—as if daring her to unlock Gerda Idun's secret.

Phigus Simenon arrived at the briefing room precisely on time, only to find that the captain was the only one there.

"Where is she?" the engineer asked brusquely.

Picard frowned. "I expect our guest and Mr. Joseph to join us at any moment. And I believe the proper protocol is 'Where is she, *sir?*' "

Simenon eyed him. "You're kidding, right? Maybe I'll call you 'sir' when you get to be twenty-nine."

The captain tried to suppress a smile, but didn't do a very good job of it. "Which will be soon. My birthday is coming up, you know."

The engineer harrumphed. "Sounds like someone is fishing for a present. Unfortunately—"

Before he could finish, the door slid aside and Joseph walked in. And there was someone behind him—someone tall, blond, and female, and well built in a human sort of way.

She also bore an uncanny resemblance to Gerda and Idun. In fact, if he hadn't known better, he would have said she *was* Gerda or Idun.

Picard got up as the woman walked into the room. He was nothing if not gallant. "Lieutenant Asmund," he said, "please have a seat."

"Thank you," the woman said.

Then she caught sight of the Gnalish.

"This is Mr. Simenon," the captain said, "our chief engineer. Mr. Simenon, Gerda Idun Asmund."

The woman stared at the engineer for a moment.

"Something wrong, Lieutenant?" Simenon asked.

Gerda Idun shook her head as she, the captain, and Joseph sat down. "No, nothing. It's just that..."

"Yes?" Simenon prompted.

"I'm sorry," she told him. "I've never met a Gnalish before, that's all."

The engineer found the remark disconcerting. "My people don't exist in your universe?"

"Oh," said Gerda Idun, "they exist. But they tend to keep to themselves. It's rare for any of them to leave Gnala."

"Actually," Joseph interjected, "that's not too far from the situation in our universe. Mr. Simenon here is only the sixth member of his species to join Starfleet."

"Fifth," Simenon said, correcting him. "But who's counting?"

Gerda Idun smiled. "In any case," she told the engineer, "it's a pleasure to meet you."

Simenon took a moment to absorb the effect of a smiling Asmund. It was amazing how different she looked from Gerda or Idun when she did that.

The captain addressed their guest. "Mr. Simenon is trying to gather as much data as he can before he attempts to formulate a theory regarding your appearance here."

Gerda Idun nodded. "I appreciate that. Obviously, I'll do anything I can to be of help."

She seemed to Simenon to possess the Asmunds' strength and sense of purpose, tempered with some of the softer human characteristics. A pleasing package, he decided—and he wasn't an easy person to please.

"All right," he said, getting down to business, "tell me everything you remember before you arrived here. Sights, smells, sounds...don't leave anything out."

Gerda Idun did as he asked. She seemed to have a good memory for details. But then, so did her counterparts.

After a few minutes, the woman appeared to run out of things to mention. She regarded Simenon hopefully. "Is that enough for you to go on?"

Of course, he had something else to go on as well— the influence of the anomaly. But the captain had asked him not to mention that to Gerda Idun.

Apparently, he still didn't trust her completely—a necessary stance, no doubt, for someone in Picard's position. But Simenon had a feeling their guest's being there was every bit the accident she claimed.

"It'll have to be," he told her. Then he turned to Picard. "If there's nothing else, I have work to do."

"You're dismissed," the captain said.

Simenon nodded his head in Gerda Idun's direction and then in Joseph's. Then he got up and left the briefing room, determined to send the woman home.

Vigo sat with his back against a wall, imprisoned with a collection of metal containers in what looked like one of the installation's storage rooms, and considered his mentor in a tawdry new light.

Obviously, Ejanix had turned traitor. For reasons Vigo desperately wished he understood, his friend had helped Kovajo and his Pandrilites seize a Starfleet installation.

Now Vigo knew why the intruders' approach hadn't been detected until it was too late. Ejanix had been working for them on the inside, tampering with sensors and door locks and maybe even using the installation's computer to jam the weapons of its security force.

He knew also why Ejanix's mood had seemed so dark. He had known what was coming and had to remain silent about it. The easiest course for him, under the circumstances, was simply to keep to himself as much as possible.

Vigo and anyone else who saw Ejanix thought he was being surly, a result of the pressure under which he'd been forced to work. But all the while, he was pursuing a separate agenda.

Vigo glanced in the direction of the open doorway, where the intruders had set up a transparent, electromagnetic barrier like the one Starfleet used in its brigs.

Like any weapons officer, he had an intimate knowledge of the way a Federation ship was constructed. Had his captors simply closed the door, he might have gained access to an EPS relay in the wall and disabled part of the installation.

But the transparent barrier prevented that. With the intruders watching him at any given time, he couldn't even consider pursuing a sabotage effort.

The weapons officer bowed his head. How foolish he had been. He should have known that something was wrong when he saw his friend acting so out of character.

But he had accepted the situation at face value, and now the entire installation was paying for his oversight.

Vigo was still berating himself when he heard his guards say something out in the corridor. A moment later, the electromagnetic barrier dropped and one of the other weapons officers went skidding into the room.

It was Sebring. And Kovajo had kept his word about punishing Vigo's colleagues. The human had taken a hard beating, if the bruises on his face were any indication.

As Vigo moved to help his comrade, the intruders put the energy barrier back up again. Sebring waved away the possibility of assistance as he got to his feet.

"Are you all right?" Vigo asked.

Sebring winced as he explored an angry welt under his eye. "I'll live."

"Did they ask you about the shuttle?"

"Uh-huh. But I didn't know what you did to it, so it was easy not to say. Have you seen Runj?"

Vigo shook his head. "No doubt, they're giving him the same kind of treatment they gave you."

"For his sake," said the human, "I hope not." He glanced through the barrier at their guards, who were monitoring their conversation. "So who are those guys?"

Vigo shrugged. "I don't know."

But that wasn't true. He knew *one* of them—and he knew also that he needed to say so. The information might prove useful to Sebring at some point.

"Actually," he amended, "Ejanix seems to be one of them. I believe he's been working with them all along."

Sebring looked at him. "Ejanix...?" He made a sound of disgust. "That must be how they got in here so easily."

Vigo nodded. "So it would appear." He sighed. "He was my friend...or so I thought."

"Some friend," said Sebring.

Vigo wanted to disagree with his colleague's tone. However, Ejanix had made it clear where his loyalties lay, and it wasn't with his former student.

The question was...why? What could possibly have compelled Ejanix to align himself with the likes of Kovajo?

The question burned in Vigo like fire.

Chapter Nine

As JOSEPH AND GERDA IDUN made their way to the mess hall, she fell silent for a moment. Then she said, "Your engineer seems to be a most thorough individual."

"He's thorough, all right," the security officer agreed. "He also happens to be one of the smartest and most resourceful people in his field."

"That's good to hear," said Gerda Idun, "considering my fate is in his hands."

Joseph looked at her, remembering her remark about the Gnalish in her universe. "So there's no Simenon on your *Stargazer?*"

"Unfortunately, no. But I wish there was. I'm sure he would be a help to us in any number of ways."

"He's certainly a help to *us,*" said Joseph. "Even if he isn't the easiest guy to get along with sometimes."

Gerda Idun laughed. "I won't tell him you said that."

"Thanks," he said. "The last thing you want to do is tick off your ship's engineer. The next thing you know, the temperature in your quarters drops sixty degrees and the intercom is piping in Vulcan love poetry."

Gerda Idun laughed again. "I've never heard any Vulcan poetry myself, but it doesn't sound appealing."

"Believe me," said Joseph, "that's an understatement."

As they continued down the corridor, he was reminded that he had been meaning to ask her something. This seemed like as good a time as any.

"Tell me," Joseph said, "is there a *me* on your ship?"

Gerda Idun looked at him. "A Pug Joseph? I'll say there is. He's the second officer, a man known for his efficiency, his resourcefulness, and his courage."

"Really?" he said. "I mean . . . wow. That's great." *Efficiency, resourcefulness, and courage.* He liked the sound of that. "I mean really *great.*"

He smiled the rest of the way to the mess hall.

Nikolas hadn't been forced to look very hard for the newest Asmund on the ship.

It was true that she didn't have a communicator badge, so the computer couldn't readily identify her whereabouts. But Joseph had been assigned to keep the woman constant company, and he very definitely had a badge.

Which was why Nikolas had decided to visit the mess hall at a time when he would normally have been getting some sleep for his next shift.

Catching sight of Joseph and his charge, the ensign

waited for his chance. He saw it when Gerda Idun left the replicator slot with her food, leaving Joseph to punch in his order.

Moving quickly and inobtrusively to the security chief's side, Nikolas said, "Lieutenant?"

Joseph turned to him. "Mr. Nikolas. How's it going?"

"Just fine," said the ensign. "But it would be going better if you could do me a favor."

The security officer looked at him askance. "What kind of favor are we talking about?"

Nikolas put his hand on Joseph's shoulder and leaned closer to him. "I would really like to get to know our transporter guest a little better."

"Gerda Idun?" Joseph chuckled. "I wouldn't get my hopes up, if I were you. If everything works out the way the captain's hoping, she won't be with us much longer."

"Even so," said Nikolas, "I'd love the chance to talk with her. What do you think?"

Joseph frowned. "I don't know. I'm not supposed to let her out of my sight."

"Then don't. Just tell her you need to speak to someone for a moment and sit down at the next table or something. It would really mean a lot to me."

The security officer shrugged. "I guess it would be all right. Just don't discuss the ship, all right? Or anything that might be considered strategic information?"

"You've got my word," Nikolas assured him.

Joseph seemed to weigh the matter a moment longer. Then he said, "Okay. You've got five minutes with her."

Nikolas saw the security officer go over to Gerda Idun and say something. Then Joseph gestured for the ensign to join them, which he did with unabashed eagerness.

"Mr. Joseph tells me you're curious about the place I come from," said Gerda Idun. "He asked me if I wouldn't mind speaking with you while he went over something with Mr. Paxton."

"And she said she wouldn't mind at all," Joseph added. "Anyway, I'll be right back."

Nikolas nodded. "Thanks." He looked at Gerda Idun as he sat down opposite her. "And thank you."

"For what?" she asked. "I haven't told you anything yet."

"For that smile you gave me in the corridor," he said. "It was the nicest one I've seen in a long time."

Gerda Idun's eyes narrowed with mock suspicion. "In my universe, that's not the kind of line that would kick off a scientific discussion."

"Well," he said, "maybe my interest in where you come from isn't entirely scientific."

"We aren't exactly shy, are we?"

"Am I offending you?"

She shook her head. "No. I like a man who's not afraid to say what's on his mind."

"That's me," he told her. "Full speed ahead and damn the photon torpedoes."

"And have you ever had occasion to regret that approach?"

"Plenty of times," Nikolas admitted. "But I'm also not the kind of person who learns from his mistakes."

Gerda Idun favored him with another smile. "We

have a saying in my universe. 'Those who fail to learn from history are doomed to repeat it.' "

"We have a similar saying at the Academy," he told her. " 'Those who fail History are doomed to repeat it.' "

She winced. "You know, that might have been the worst joke I've ever heard."

He shrugged. "They can't all be gems."

"With that kind of attitude, you'll never make captain."

"If I were the captain," he said, "I'd be up on the bridge right now, making decisions that could affect the lives of the entire crew. I'm much happier right where I am."

Gerda Idun laughed. "You're a very silly man."

"Who's not afraid to say what's on his mind. And you like that, remember?"

She laughed again. "Yes, I like that."

They talked a little while longer—about Nikolas mostly, as it turned out—but it wasn't all silliness. He told her about Earth, how and where he grew up, and the trouble he'd had fitting in at the Academy.

Every so often, when the conversation got a little *too* serious, he made her laugh again. After all, it was her smile that had drawn him to her in the first place.

Finally, after considerably more than five minutes, the most generous Pug Joseph came over and told Nikolas his business with Paxton had been resolved.

The ensign nodded, however reluctantly. As he got up, he turned to Gerda Idun. "It was great talking with you. We'll have to do it again sometime."

Her eyes seemed to lose their focus for a second, as if she had just remembered something important. Then she met his gaze again and said, "You know where to find me."

He did indeed.

The *Stargazer*'s weapons officer had paced his prison perhaps a hundred times before the guards finally lowered the barrier and threw Runj inside.

Vigo and Sebring moved to the Vobilite's side. Like his colleagues before him, Runj had been worked over thoroughly, his face a mask of dark red bruises.

"They asked me about the shuttle," he rasped, a swollen lip joining his tusks as an impediment to speech.

"I know," said Vigo, regretting what Runj had gone through. "They asked Sebring and me as well."

"Whatever you did to it," Sebring told the Pandrilite, "it must be driving them crazy."

Their captors couldn't even transmit any classified data to their mother ship—not with the magnetic-storm layer raging above them. It gave Vigo a small measure of satisfaction that they had stymied the intruders, but it didn't make up for the pain Sebring and Runj had endured.

The human cast a glance at their guards. "What do you think they're going to do next?"

Vigo knew what he meant. The intruders had gone through all three of them and failed to get what they needed. They would have to step up their efforts.

And as the one who had carried out the sabotage, he was the one on whom they would most likely focus their attentions.

"I don't know," he said, in answer to Sebring's question. But he had a feeling he would find out.

Nikolas was on his way to the bridge to take his turn at Vigo's weapons console when he heard a familiar voice call his name.

Turning, he saw Obal hustling to catch up with him. "Hey, buddy," the ensign said, slowing his pace, "what's the good word?"

He was surprised at how cheerful he sounded. But then, he had reason to be that way.

"Nikolas," said Obal, as he finally pulled up alongside his friend, "I've been looking for you."

"How come?"

"I wanted to speak with you about Lieutenant Asmund. That is, the Lieutenant Asmund who beamed aboard."

Nikolas shrugged. "What about her?"

"I stopped by the mess hall earlier on my way to security and saw you talking to her. She was *laughing*—apparently, at something you had just said."

"Is there a regulation against laughing?" the ensign asked good-naturedly. "Because if there is, I think even the captain might have violated it."

Obal sighed. "You know there's no such regulation. And it isn't the laughter itself that makes me concerned. It's what it could lead to."

Nikolas was touched that his pal was looking out for him. But as usual, Obal was going a little overboard.

"My friend," said the security officer, "are you certain that it's wise to become friendly with this woman?"

Nikolas laughed. "Obal, I just *talked* to her."

"Yes," the Binderian conceded. "And Romeo merely *talked* to Juliet."

Nikolas looked at him. "How do you know about Romeo and Juliet?"

"Lieutenant Kastiigan recommended the play to me. He saw it in San Francisco, when he was at the Academy."

Nikolas chuckled. "Really."

"He told me it was a most engaging drama, one of the best he had ever seen performed. He especially admired the ending, in which the lovers perish."

"Sounds like Kastiigan," said Nikolas, stopping at a turbolift station and tapping the metal plate beside it.

Obal stopped too. "But it is not Lieutenant Kastiigan I am worried about. It is *you.*"

The ensign dismissed the idea with a wave of his hand. "There's no reason to worry, pal. She's not Gerda or Idun. She's from another universe, for godsakes."

"Which is exactly my point," Obal said. "You do not know her very well. Your attraction to her cannot be anything but a physical one."

Nikolas was about to ask his friend what was wrong with *that*. But before he could get the words out, he realized Obal was wrong. It *wasn't* just a physical attraction.

Sure, it might have started out that way. But somewhere in those few short minutes they'd had in the mess hall, it had become something more than that.

"Listen," he said, "I appreciate your concern. But don't worry. I've got everything under control."

"I don't think—" Obal started to protest.

But before he could finish, the turbolift doors opened, revealing a compartment full of ship's personnel.

"Sorry," said Nikolas, backing into the lift. "Gotta run." And with a wave of apology, he watched the sliding doors cut off his view of a very frustrated-looking Binderian.

Gerda circled to her left, her open hands moving in front of her, her legs spread shoulder-wide for balance—while directly in front of her, Idun did precisely the same thing.

It wasn't unusual for them to opt for the same stance in their sparring sessions there in the gym. In fact, Gerda would have been surprised if they had *not* occasionally opted for the same stance.

After all, they had been trained by the same man—their adopted father, who over a lifetime had made himself an expert at a variety of Klingon martial arts. As a result, their strategies were the same, their execution was the same—even their weaknesses tended to be the same.

That was what made their sparring sessions so intriguing for Gerda. It wasn't like fighting an enemy so much as it was like fighting herself.

Unfortunately, she couldn't enjoy the exercise as much as she usually did. She still had Gerda Idun on her mind, and she couldn't seem to stop thinking about the woman no matter how hard she tried.

"W'heiya!" Idun snarled suddenly, and launched a fist at her sister's face.

It wasn't Idun's best move—far from it—and yet Gerda only narrowly avoided it. And when she tried to strike back with a series of kicks, Idun danced out of the way almost effortlessly.

Gerda bit her lip and resolved to do better.

Moving into a *dafakh'rit* posture—her adopted father's favorite—she came at Idun with one hand held high and the other low. When she got within striking range, she kicked at her sister's chin and followed with a long high-hand jab.

But Idun took a step back at just the right moment and both blows fell short of their target. Obviously, she had seen the sequence coming.

Again, Gerda executed the maneuver, attempting to put more snap into it. But again, her sister had no trouble slipping out of harm's way.

Gerda was about to try a different approach when Idun dropped her hands and came out of her stance. "All right," she said. "What's the problem?"

"Problem?" Gerda echoed.

"Your heart is not in this—it hasn't been since we got here. So what's the problem?"

Gerda hadn't thought her lack of concentration was that obvious. But now that Idun had called her on it, what course would be wiser to take?

Should I tell her the truth? the navigator asked herself. *Should I say that I was preoccupied with Gerda Idun and the duplicity I saw in her?*

But really, what could she say? That she had noticed something Idun could have noticed just as easily, but somehow didn't? It would sound as if Gerda were making it up—as if she were jealous of Gerda Idun, perhaps.

And she *wasn't* jealous. Definitely not.

Clearly, the woman had changed the dynamic between Gerda and her sister, if only subtly. But that didn't mean that Gerda was jealous. She was merely following her instincts, as she had been trained to do.

The more the navigator thought about it, the less inclined she was to discuss the matter. Perhaps later, when she had something more concrete to speak of. But not now.

"It's nothing," she said. "I just need to concentrate." And she lowered herself into a crouch.

Idun scrutinized her twin for a moment, as if trying to decide whether to believe her. Then she dropped into a crouch as well. Slowly, she began circling to her right.

Forcing herself to focus on the task at hand, Gerda circled in the same direction. Then she drew her hand back and assumed the *kave'ragh* stance in preparation for an attack.

But before she could launch it, the door to the gym hissed open and admitted two familiar figures. One was Pug Joseph. The other was his constant companion, Gerda Idun, who had changed into a set of borrowed exercise togs.

Idun was facing away from the door, so she didn't see who had come in right away. But she must have noticed something in her sister's eyes because she looked back over her shoulder.

"Sorry," Gerda Idun said, raising her hands as a token of her regret. "I didn't mean to interrupt."

Too late, Gerda thought.

"You're not interrupting," Idun told their look-alike. "We were just getting under way. In fact, you're welcome to take part if you like."

Gerda felt a surge of resentment. No one had ever taken part in their sparring sessions except her and her sister.

As if in response, Idun glanced at her. "That is," she added, "if Gerda doesn't mind."

Under the circumstances, how could the navigator say no? "Of course not," she said, trying to keep the rancor out of her voice.

Gerda Idun smiled at Idun's suggestion. "I'd love to, but I don't know any Klingon martial arts. That's what you were doing, wasn't it?"

"We were," said Idun. "But it's all right. We'll go easy on you."

Gerda Idun turned to Joseph. "All right with you?"

"I don't see why not," the security officer told her.

Gerda Idun turned back to the helm officer. "All right," she said. "You're on."

"Good," said Idun. Again, she glanced at Gerda. "Would you like to go first?"

Gerda shook her head. "You go. I'll watch."

Turning back to their look-alike, Idun assumed a *chok'tiyan* position, which kept both her elbows close to her body to emphasize defense. "Go ahead," she said. "I'm ready."

Gerda Idun raised her fists and spread her feet apart, one ahead of the other. Then she approached her opponent with small, careful steps.

This won't take long, Gerda thought.

Gerda Idun had no idea what she was up against. Idun would soon grow tired of playing with her and find an excuse to end the match gracefully.

Or so the navigator thought—until their guest advanced behind a series of blinding-quick blows. They were so powerful, so accurate, Idun barely managed to ward them off.

Before the helm officer could gather herself, Gerda Idun pressed her attack, launching punches in devastating combinations. Finally, one of her assaults landed, catching Idun in the shoulder. Then a second one dealt Idun a glancing blow to the head.

Gerda was shocked. Their counterpart seemed so polite, so reserved, and she hadn't had the benefit of growing up in a warrior culture. It was hard to imagine her pushing Idun to the limits of her skill.

And yet, that was exactly what Gerda Idun was doing.

Finally, Idun seemed to adapt to her look-alike's style. She blocked blow after devastating blow as if she had figured out in advance where they were going to land. Then, little by little, she started to turn the tide.

But it wasn't easy. Gerda Idun gave ground grudgingly, fighting her adversary every inch of the way. Her expression had changed a good deal since the match began; it was a mask of grim determination now, virtually indistinguishable from Idun's.

Gerda felt her stomach muscles tighten into a knot. *Finish her,* she found herself crying out in the privacy of her mind. *Finish her* now.

Finally, Idun did the last thing Gerda Idun would have expected—she dropped to the mat, planted her hand there, and swept her counterpart's feet out from under her. Then, as Gerda Idun unceremoniously hit the floor, Idun lashed out with her foot at her opponent's face.

Idun could have broken her adversary's neck if she

had followed through with the blow. As it was, she stopped perhaps an inch from Gerda Idun's chin.

For a moment, the newcomer stared at Idun's heel, her chest rising and falling with the intensity of her effort. Then she began to laugh—and it wasn't the kind of halfhearted chuckle that came out of most humans. It was a lusty laugh, a laugh worthy of a warrior.

As Gerda looked on, her sister began to laugh too. Springing to her feet, she reached down and clasped Gerda Idun's hand. Then she hauled her opponent off the mat.

"Well fought," said Idun.

Gerda Idun nodded and brushed a stray lock of hair off her forehead. "Thanks. You too."

Gerda cursed silently. It wasn't enough that the stranger had won Idun's sympathy. Now, it seemed, she had won Idun's respect as well.

"So much for nature versus nurture," Joseph remarked appreciatively. "It looks like those fighting skills were in the Asmund genes all along."

Idun shrugged and cast a conspiratorial look at Gerda Idun. "Perhaps," she allowed.

The newcomer clapped Idun on the shoulder and turned to Gerda. "She's all yours."

The irony of the comment wasn't lost on the navigator. "Thank you," she said, "but I don't feel much like sparring anymore." With a glance at her sister, she left the gym.

But even before the doors hissed closed behind her, Gerda knew she had made a fool of herself. She had acted like a petulant child, not a full-grown woman—

and certainly not like an officer on a Federation starship.

Unfortunately, it was too late to take back her behavior, and she couldn't bring herself to apologize for it—not to a woman who wasn't what she seemed. So she kept on going, down the corridor and into the turbolift.

And she didn't stop until she reached her quarters.

Chapter Ten

As PICARD ENTERED engineering, he saw Simenon working at a sleek, black console in the shadow of the warp reactor. Crossing the room, the captain joined him.

"Mr. Simenon," he said as he approached, "you wished to speak with me?"

"I did," the Gnalish confirmed without looking up. "Take a look at this, will you?"

What Picard saw, when he peeked over Simenon's shoulder at his monitor, was a blue-on-black grid overrun by a swarm of yellow dots—all of them emanating from a larger yellow configuration in the corner of the screen.

"The dots," said the engineer, "represent the influence of the anomaly. As you can see, it's one hell of a powerfully charged system—one that can turn a simple ship-to-ship transport into a much more unusual event."

"Like a transit from one universe to another."

"Indeed," said Simenon.

Picard nodded. "So it's as we suspected—the anomaly is the culprit in this case."

"Mind you," said Simenon, "I can't say that for certain. But I've ruled out every other explanation. Under the circumstances, I think we'd be wise to go with this one."

The captain looked at his engineer. "And in terms of reversing the process?"

Simenon shrugged his narrow shoulders beneath his lab coat. "All we have to go by is the *Enterprise*'s experience. They got their captain and his officers back by remaining in the presence of that ion storm."

Picard saw where the Gnalish was going. "So if we want to send Gerda Idun back—"

"We'll have to do it in the presence of the anomaly," said Simenon, "or find one just like it. And you know what the odds of that are."

"I see," said the captain.

"Fortunately," the engineer added, "our shields are a match for the anomaly's radiation output. So, theoretically, we can stay here indefinitely without endangering the crew."

"Theoretically," Picard echoed.

But that only took into account the anomaly. And in time, another sort of danger would likely rear its head.

"Of course," said Simenon, "I'll need to make some alterations to one of the transporter systems. Lieutenant Asmund got here in one piece only through sheer, dumb luck. For her to get *back* in one piece, she'll need some help."

The captain nodded. "How long do you expect these alterations to take?"

Simenon made a face. "Did they ask da Vinci how long it would take to paint the Mona Lisa?"

Picard frowned at him.

"A day or so," said the Gnalish, "assuming I'm not asked to fix some EPS relay in the meantime."

The captain assured him that there weren't any EPS repairs in the offing. Then he left Simenon to do his work.

Vigo paced the storage room in which he and his colleagues had been imprisoned, still wrestling with the question of why his friend had become a traitor.

It didn't make sense to him. He and Ejanix had been raised in the same enlightened society. They had been exposed to the same high-minded cultural values.

For that matter, the intruders had been exposed to them too. Yet they seemed to have forgotten what their elders taught them back on Pandril. Otherwise, they would neither have coveted someone else's technology nor considered the use of violence in obtaining it.

And in Ejanix's case, it wasn't just Pandrilite culture that relegated against what he had done. It was the fact that he was an officer in Starfleet.

His superiors at Starfleet Command had placed their trust in him. They had given him whatever he needed to make use of his talents. And somehow, he had found the audacity to throw it back in their faces.

Vigo could never have imagined that his friendship with Ejanix would come to this. A part of him simply refused to accept it. And yet, he had seen the evidence of his mentor's treachery with his own eyes.

"Someone's coming," Runj snapped.

Vobilites were known for their keen sense of hearing. But when Vigo concentrated, he could hear it too—the clatter of boot heels on the floor outside their prison.

Someone was coming, all right. The Pandrilite exchanged glances with Sebring and Runj, wondering what it meant. Another beating, perhaps?

A moment later, the footsteps arrived outside their open door. But when their guards deactivated the transparent barrier and stepped aside, it wasn't Kovajo they admitted into the room.

It was Ejanix.

Once, Vigo would have known exactly what to expect of him. Now, he couldn't begin to guess.

Ejanix considered Sebring and Runj, who looked back at him with battered faces. Then his gaze fell on Vigo and remained there for a moment.

Finally, Ejanix walked over to his former student and said, "How are you?"

"I've been better," said Vigo.

"You shouldn't have sabotaged that shuttle," Ejanix told him. "That was a mistake."

"It was my duty as a Starfleet officer to keep your friends from stealing what's stored here."

"Is that all you can see?" Ejanix asked, his forehead ridging over. "Your obligations to the aliens' Starfleet?"

Vigo looked at him wonderingly. "The *aliens'* Starfleet? And not *yours?*"

133

"I thought it was mine when I worked at the Academy. But I've since learned otherwise."

"From Kovajo?" Vigo asked.

Ejanix stiffened a bit. "Him...and others like him."

Vigo shook his head. "I don't understand. What could they have said to you that would make you become a traitor to the Federation?"

His mentor looked as if he had eaten something rancid. "I call myself a rebel, not a traitor."

"A rebel?" Vigo echoed. "What is there for a Pandrilite to rebel against?"

"A great deal," said Ejanix. "Our society and everything it has come to represent."

Vigo shook his head. "What are you saying? For the first time in ages, everything on Pandril is in balance. The modern era has been hailed as a golden age."

"Because our people devote themselves to the Three Virtues—Humility, Selflessness, and Stoicism."

"That's right."

Ejanix made a sound of derision. "Spoken like a true member of the Elevated Castes."

Vigo hadn't expected that sort of comment. "What has my caste got to do with it?"

"It may appear that there is balance from your narrow, patrician point of view. But if you come down to the catacomb levels, down to the place where the Lesser Castes live, you will see that Pandril is in disarray. Every day is an injustice, tolerable only to those who perpetrate it."

The weapons officer didn't understand. "If there are injustices, then why not petition the council to correct them?"

"The council is already aware of them," said Ejanix. "The councilors, in their unassailable wisdom, simply choose to look the other way."

"That's difficult to believe," Vigo told him. "Those who serve on the council—"

"Are supposed to be beyond reproach," said Ejanix. "I *know* that. *Every* Pandrilite knows that. But the councilors are not what you think. They exist only to preserve the status quo, which serves the purposes of the Elevated Castes—and frustrates the ambitions of the Lesser ones.

"And the Virtues are just like the council—pillars of What Is, bars against What Might Be. It's easy to ask others to remain humble, to remain selfless, and to endure hardship, when you need never worry about doing so yourself."

Vigo shook his head. "This doesn't sound like you, Ejanix. It sounds like some deluded malcontent."

"I *am* a malcontent," his friend said without hesitation. "But you're the one who's deluded, Vigo. You should go back to Pandril and take a look around. Take a *good* look. You may see what I'm talking about."

The lieutenant considered Ejanix's words. He had never known his mentor to be unstable. But the way he was speaking, contrary to everything Vigo had ever understood or believed in...

"It doesn't matter," he told Ejanix finally. "Even if what you say were true, it doesn't give you the right to betray Starfleet. You took an oath just as I did."

Ejanix's mouth twisted. "And for a long time, I felt bound by that oath. Then I learned the truth." He leaned closer to his former pupil, his eyes blazing with righteous indignation. "How could I remain loyal to Starfleet when it was part of the system that was holding me down? When it was a critical component in the machine of Lesser Caste oppression?"

There was no such oppression, Vigo insisted inwardly. But it was obvious that Ejanix didn't want to hear that.

"So you've thrown in with Kovajo," he concluded, "and others who think as he does. And you've discarded the Virtues for a nobler ideal."

"That's right," Ejanix told him, putting his hand on Vigo's shoulder. "And I want you to join us."

The weapons officer hadn't expected that. "That's why you're here," he said as realization dawned. "To try to turn me against Starfleet as well."

And then to find out what I did to your shuttle, he added silently.

Ejanix shook his head. "You're looking at it all wrong, Vigo. You won't just be turning away from something. You'll be turning *toward* something—the kind of justice that Pandril has never known."

Vigo turned his head so his mentor could see the bruises on his cheek. "Take a good look, Ejanix. Is this justice? Do I deserve the punishment Kovajo was so quick to mete out?"

Ejanix frowned, but he didn't seem to have an answer.

The weapons officer pressed on. "Or is it possible," he asked, "that Kovajo isn't as interested in justice as he is in being on top for a change?"

Ejanix's frown deepened. "It's not that way at all. Kovajo is working on behalf of all of us."

"All of us?" Vigo echoed. "Or all of the rebels who follow him toward his idea of a better society?"

His mentor looked frustrated. "You don't understand."

"Then *help* me to understand," said Vigo. "Tell me what Kovajo plans to do with the technology he's stolen."

Ejanix glanced at the doorway and the guards who were standing there. Then he looked back.

"He's not going to build any weapons himself," the engineer said in a conspiratorial tone. "He's going to sell the designs to raise money for the revolution."

"Even if that's true," said Vigo, "he's putting weapons in the hands of those who may wish to hurt innocent people. Sentient beings will die on some planet you've never heard of so Kovajo can finance his rebellion on Pandril."

Vigo's mentor looked surprised. Obviously, he hadn't thought about that.

"And will it be a *bloodless* rebellion, Ejanix? Is that what Kovajo has told you—just as he said your venture here on Wayland Prime would be bloodless? Or will lives be sacrificed on our homeworld as well?"

Touching his fingertips to the cut above his eye, the weapons officer showed his friend the thin, wet smear of gore on them. "Kovajo seems willing to spill vast quantities of this to get what he wants. Are *you?*"

The older Pandrilite looked as if he had been slapped across the face. For a moment, it seemed to Vigo that Ejanix was going to respond to his protégé's charges.

But he didn't. Without speaking a single additional word, he turned around and walked back across the room. He didn't even acknowledge the guards at the door as he went past them and disappeared from sight.

The weapons officer felt a pang of disappointment. For a moment there, he had believed he was making progress. It was clear to him now that he had been mistaken.

Ejanix was too set on rebellion to listen to reason. If Vigo were to stop Kovajo from getting away with his scheme, he would have to find another way.

As Gerda entered sickbay, she was relieved to see that all the biobeds were empty. That meant there was only one person present—the one she had come to see.

Heading straight for Greyhorse's office, she entered without knocking. The doctor was sitting at his desk, consulting his monitor in some medical matter.

He looked up at her, then automatically peered past her at the rest of sickbay—as if to see if anyone would notice a brief liaison. But that wasn't why the navigator had come to see him.

"I need to talk," Gerda said.

Greyhorse looked at her, clearly a little surprised. But then, she had never said anything like that to him before. In fact, she had seldom said it to anybody, Idun included.

"About what?" he asked.

She closed the door to his office, but declined to sit in the room's only other chair. "About Gerda Idun."

The doctor's surprise turned to concern. "Is there something wrong with her?"

Gerda shook her head. "She's fine. In perfect health. In fact, she just acquitted herself rather well against Idun in the gym."

Greyhorse looked confused. "Then what's the problem?"

She looked at him. "Gerda Idun may have acquitted herself well, but I did not."

Seeing that the doctor's confusion had only increased, she started at the beginning. She told him about the look she had seen in Gerda Idun's eyes, her sister's seemingly blind acceptance of the woman, and the childish way she had acted in the gym.

"I embarrassed myself," Gerda said. "I made myself an object of scorn. And I still haven't recovered sufficiently to look Idun in the face."

Greyhorse nodded. "I see. But why *did* you act that way in the gym? It's almost as if you were…"

"Yes?" she said. "Go ahead and say it. As if I were *jealous* of Gerda Idun."

"But," said the doctor, "that's…ridiculous." He turned away from her to resume his work. "I mean…how could you *possibly* be jealous of her?"

Gerda frowned as she recalled the incident in the gymnasium. "You haven't seen the way Idun acts when she's around. It's as if Gerda Idun is her sister, her confidante, and I'm…I don't know what. Something else."

The doctor looked back over his shoulder at her, a look of distraction on his face. As it cleared, he said, "Right. I see how that could be a problem."

For the first time, Gerda noticed that his cheeks were redder than usual. But why would he be blushing? Unless…

The more she thought about it, the more sense it made. Gerda Idun looked just like her. But unlike Gerda or her sister, Gerda Idun had been raised by humans.

That made her more like Greyhorse as well. And

men—human or Klingon—were timid creatures at heart. Few of them liked to venture far afield when it came to matters of the heart.

Gerda lifted her chin. "It seems there is a bigger problem than the one I came here to tell you about."

Greyhorse's brow gathered in a knot above the bridge of his nose. "What do you mean?"

She made a sound of disgust. "You prefer her to me, don't you? Because she's human. Because she won't leave marks on your flesh when she makes love to you."

The doctor's Adam's apple climbed his throat and descended again. "You're mistaken," he insisted. "I haven't got the slightest interest in her."

"Liar," Gerda spat. "I can see it in your eyes. She would be the best of both worlds for you, wouldn't she?"

"Gerda," Greyhorse protested, "I—"

She didn't let him finish. With a last seething glance in his direction, she made her way out of his office and then out of sickbay—her stomach churning at the thought that she had lost not only her sister's affection, but her lover's as well.

Chapter Eleven

THE FIRST THING Nikolas noticed when he walked into the *Stargazer*'s lounge was Gerda Idun—or, more accurately, the back of Gerda Idun's head.

The second thing he noticed was Joseph, who was sitting across a low table from Gerda Idun. His expression indicated that their conversation wasn't an especially jovial one.

Someone else might have taken that as a sign that his company might not be appreciated. But then, Nikolas had been barging in where he wasn't wanted all his life. He saw no reason to diverge from that policy now.

As he approached the pair, Joseph looked up at him. But he didn't give the ensign any sign that he wasn't welcome there. In fact, Joseph looked almost relieved.

Gerda Idun cast a glance back at Nikolas as well. Like the security chief, she seemed glad to see him.

"We meet again," the ensign told her.

"Quite a coincidence," she noted.

Nikolas turned to Joseph, making a silent request for some time alone with Gerda Idun—or, rather, as alone as Joseph could let her get.

The security officer frowned. Then he said, "I think I need to speak with Mr. Paxton again."

Neither Nikolas nor Gerda Idun pointed out that Paxton wasn't there, or that Joseph hadn't expressed any need to speak with the man before. They just let the remark go by.

As Joseph moved to the other side of the room and tapped his combadge, Nikolas took the seat opposite Gerda Idun's. Then he said, "Everything all right?"

She shrugged. "I'm not sure. I walked into the gym before and saw my counterparts sparring. Idun asked me if I wanted to take part, and before I knew it she and I were going at it."

Nikolas grimaced. He had gone at it with Idun himself, and come out very much on the losing end.

"You don't *look* battered," he said.

"I wasn't. But when we were done, Gerda seemed angry with us—and with *me* in particular, I think. But I didn't go in there intending to interrupt them. It was Idun's idea."

The ensign considered the matter. "That doesn't sound like Gerda. She's usually pretty much in control."

"Maybe I just hit a nerve," said Gerda Idun. "Oh well. Idun didn't seem to think it was anything irreparable."

"And who would know better than she would?"

She smiled. "You always know the right thing to say, don't you?"

"Always," he said. "I just have this habit of saying the wrong thing instead."

"Which is why your career hasn't been as sparkling as it might have been. Or so you claim."

Nikolas leaned forward in his chair. "You've got a better explanation?"

"It sounds to me," she said, "like you've been sabotaging yourself—like you're a bit intimidated by the prospect of taking responsibility for people, so you're making sure that possibility never materializes."

He smiled back at her. "You told me you were an engineer, but it seems you've also got the makings of a counselor."

"Is that a compliment?"

"That depends," he said, "on what you think of counselors. Personally, I think every ship should have one."

Gerda Idun looked skeptical. "You do?"

"Absolutely," he told her, "if they're all as easy on the eyes as you are."

Not that the odds of that were very good. Every counselor Nikolas had ever met—including those who had counseled him at the Academy—was short, dumpy, and balding.

Gerda Idun laughed. "You just don't stop, do you?"

She seemed to be enjoying his company every bit as much as he was enjoying hers. He found that surprising in light of the way Gerda and Idun looked at him.

Or *didn't* look at him, to be more accurate about it.

Supposedly, Gerda Idun had the same genetic makeup they did. And yet, she had seemed to have a soft spot for Nikolas ever since the moment she saw him in the corridor.

Funny how that worked....

And then it hit him: She was from another universe—one that seemed to parallel Nikolas's pretty closely. And if there was a Gerda Idun Asmund in that universe...

"Can I ask you a question?" he said.

"Sure. What is it?"

"Is there an Andreas Nikolas where you come from?"

The light in her eyes seemed to dim.

Not good, he thought. "What?" he asked softly.

"There is indeed an Andreas Nikolas in my universe," Gerda Idun told him, looking down at her hands all of a sudden. "Or rather...there *was*."

The ensign got an eerie feeling hearing her say that. It was a little like attending his own funeral.

"What happened to him?" he asked. But it felt as if he were really asking, "What happened to *me?*"

"He died," she said. "In an accident."

He heard a catch in her voice as she imparted the information. It led him to believe that Gerda Idun and his counterpart were more than mere acquaintances.

Before he could ask, his companion filled him in. "We were just teenagers at the time, but we had the beginnings of a serious relationship. Unfortunately, it never had a chance to develop into something deeper."

"I'm sorry," he said.

Gerda Idun tried to smile, but there was a liquid shimmer in her eyes that told Nikolas she still hadn't gotten over the tragedy. "I never got to see him as he would have been," she said, "as an adult. Until *now.*"

So that's what she sees in me, he thought. *That's been the attraction all along. I remind her of her dead lover.*

Nikolas would have expected something like that to bother him. After all, he had been jealous of other guys from time to time. Why not himself?

But it *didn't* bother him—not even a little bit. He found he didn't care why Gerda Idun had feelings for him. All that mattered to him was that she *did.*

"You know," he said, smiling, "you've been given a chance most people don't have. You can find out what might have happened between you and that teenager."

She averted her eyes, as if she were ashamed of herself. "Don't think I haven't thought about that."

Nikolas studied her face. "And?"

"With any luck," said Gerda Idun, "I'm going to return to my own universe and leave you here in this one. It doesn't make sense to start something that's doomed to end."

He didn't like the sound of that. However, her tone wasn't one of finality. It seemed to the ensign that there was some tiny bit of wiggle room.

And that was all he had ever asked for.

Wutor Qiyuntor eyed the phenomenon to which his Middle Order overseers had dispatched him. It was long, violet in color, and—if his ship's data collectors could be believed—was generating an enormous number of charged particles.

The commander eyed the numbers crawling by at the bottom of his viewscreen and waited for the right moment. Finally, he turned to his pilot.

"One-quarter light-speed," he told Jeglen.

Instantly, the *Ekhonarid* slowed to a crawl, the streaks of brightness on Wutor's viewscreen diminishing drastically in length. But then, they were within twenty-five million kilometers of the phenomenon. There was no longer any need for haste.

Wutor leaned back in his brace. All he could do now was wait—and pray that an enemy arrived before the High Order squadron summoned by the overseers.

"Commander," said Delakan, the female who stood at the data-collection panel. Her face was caught in its pale green glare. "There's someone else here."

Wutor felt his neck pulse accelerate. "What do you mean?" he demanded.

"Another vessel," Delakan elaborated. She looked up at the viewscreen, which gave no indication of any other ships in the vicinity. "It's hiding behind the phenomenon."

The commander leaned forward in his brace, the flat teeth in the back of his mouth grinding as he considered the phenomenon. *"Show* me."

A moment later, the viewscreen abandoned its visual perspective on the phenomenon and replaced it with an augmented thermal-trace graphic—one that represented the other vessel as a ghostly, red shape on an otherwise unbroken field of blue.

Wutor's tongue snaked over his teeth. Delakan was right. The ship was using the phenomenon to mask its presence.

And it wasn't a Balduk ship. He could tell even from this crudest and quickest of scans. It was an invader— here, in a part of space claimed by the Balduk.

The very thought made his blood boil.

But he kept his head. After all, he didn't want to merely engage this enemy. He wanted to crush it and drag its carcass back to the homeworld as evidence of his victory.

When he stood in the brace of a High Order vessel, he would simply have swooped in with his subordinate ships and seized the victory. But to his shame, he was no longer in command of a High Order vessel.

All he had to work with was the *Ekhonarid*. But if he used his brain, that would be enough.

"Run a full scan," he told Delakan.

"Aye," she said, and bent to the task.

Wutor could feel his nails digging into his palms. Patience had never been his best attribute. But he would exercise it if it meant a chance to regain his stature.

As Delakan worked, the commander heard the grinding of an ascent compartment. Even without turning from the screen, he knew who was in it.

Tsioveth swore as she left the compartment and advanced to Wutor's side. "Then it's true," she said, her eyes alight with the Balduk urge to battle.

"How are the plasma conduits on weapons deck?" the commander asked with a sneer.

His mechanic craved victory as much as Wutor or anyone else aboard the *Ekhonarid*. He knew her answer would be with tinged with optimism.

"They'll hold," she said.

Wutor could have used a little more optimism than *that*. "They'd better. We'll soon have need of them."

"Scan complete," Delakan reported.

As she said it, another graphic went up on the screen,

replacing the first one. This time, it wasn't a red image on the blue background—it was a yellow one. And it clearly described a spacegoing vessel with a flat circular section and four long, skinny appendages.

Wutor wasn't an expert on alien designs, but even he knew a Federation ship when he saw one.

A Federation vessel in Balduk territory, the commander thought, bristling with anger and indignation. Something would have to be done about that, and quickly.

"Energy to weapons," he ordered.

"Energy to weapons," said Potrepo, a vibration of excitement in his voice.

And why wouldn't there be? All Balduk longed for battle. All Balduk yearned for the chance to defend their people's borders. Potrepo, old as he might be, was really no different from anyone else.

"They're charged," the weaponer reported.

Wutor studied the graphic on the viewscreen. The Federation invader wasn't moving. Obviously, he didn't fear the *Ekhonarid.* But her commander would give the invader *reason* to fear her.

"The enemy is attemping to contact us," said Wutor's communications technician.

Wutor laughed, the harsh sound of it echoing throughout his bridge. What could the enemy say that could possibly be of interest to him?

"They'll receive no reply," he said, "other than the lash of our weapons!"

Gerda was striding down the corridor outside sickbay, still stinging from what she had seen in Greyhorse's eyes, when she saw her sister coming from the other direction.

She wasn't alone either. Gerda Idun was with her. And so, naturally, was Pug Joseph.

Gerda wished she could have turned and gone back the other way, but it was too late. Idun and the others had already caught sight of her.

Fine, she thought. *I'll face this like a warrior, the same way I would face anything else.*

Fortunately, her sister made it easier for her. She greeted Gerda as if nothing had happened.

"Come," she said. "We're on our way to stellar cartography."

Joseph elaborated. "Gerda Idun doesn't have anything like it on her *Stargazer.*"

Gerda Idun, the navigator thought, *can go straight to Gre'thor.* The last thing she wanted to do was give tours to someone whose motives she didn't trust.

But Gerda couldn't say that. Not without embarrassing herself even further.

So, as much as it galled her, as much as it ate at her like a slow-acting Klingon poison, she tamped down her suspicions and her resentment. And without a word, she fell in line with Gerda Idun's entourage.

The physical act was predictably easy. Not so the task of containing her emotions. With each step Gerda took, she could feel shame and anger roil inside her.

Up ahead of her, her sister and Gerda Idun walked side by side, identical but for the clothing they wore. Every so often, they said something to each other—just a word or two, but it seemed to be enough.

Gerda imagined that she and Idun had looked like that once. But it was no longer just she and Idun. Now, as repugnant as she found the idea, there were three of them.

Three.

Dammit, she *was* jealous—just as she had told Greyhorse. She was aflame with it. But it wasn't jealousy that made her believe Gerda Idun was deceiving them.

There was more to it. The navigator was certain of that. And she clung to that certainty all the while her jealousy was writhing inside her like spoiled bloodwine.

She was so preoccupied with her inner turmoil, so focused on it, she didn't notice most of the crewmen passing her in the corridor in groups of two and three. But as she passed a particular group, something caught her eye.

It was a look—a sliding of eyes in her direction. As she looked more closely, drawn forcibly from her private dialogue, she saw that the eyes belonged to Lieutenant Refsland.

And she remembered Idun's comment about the transporter operator's fantasies. *Refsland is probably imagining what it would be like to have sex with us....*

The next thing Gerda knew, she had the man pinned against the bulkhead, his tunic bunched in her fist.

"What are you doing?" Refsland asked.

"You were staring at me," Gerda snarled, unable to control herself.

Refsland shook his head. "I wasn't doing anything of the sort."

"Yes, you were," she insisted.

"Gerda," said her sister, putting her hand on Gerda's shoulder. "You can't—"

"I *can*," said Gerda. "I've had enough of this."

"Whoa," said Joseph, trying to wedge himself between the navigator and Refsland. "Calm down, Lieutenant."

But she didn't *want* to calm down. She wanted to lash out at someone. She wanted to vent all the anger and resentment that had been building inside her.

"Calm down," Joseph repeated earnestly, "or I swear, I'll throw you in the brig!"

Suddenly, Gerda felt the deck buck under her feet, forcing her to clutch at a bulkhead for support. Her sister, Joseph, and Gerda Idun all did the same.

"What's going on?" Gerda Idun asked.

"Battle stations!" came the captain's voice. "All senior bridge officers, report on the double!"

Suddenly, Gerda's anger cooled. It was as if she had been dipped in a glacial stream, all negative emotions leached out of her.

She didn't give any more thought to Refsland or Gerda Idun, or any of her other sources of frustration. She just bolted for the nearest turbolift, absolutely certain that her sister was right behind her.

Chapter Twelve

PICARD GRABBED the armrests on his command chair as a second Balduk volley wracked the *Stargazer*.

"Shields down twenty-two percent," Kochman reported from his post at the navigation console.

"No significant damage to the ship," said Ulelo from the com station.

Fortunately, they had gotten their deflectors up before the Balduk vessel could land any serious blows. But with the enemy on their tail, they were still at a disadvantage.

Suddenly, the turbolift doors opened and Picard's senior officers flooded the bridge. *Finally,* he thought. If he was going to get anywhere with the Balduk, he stood a better chance of it with his best people in place.

As he watched, Idun and Gerda took over at helm and

navigation. Paxton replaced the ensign at the com station, Kastiigan appeared at the science panel, and Simenon assumed control of the engineering console.

Only Vigo was missing, Ensign Nikolas serving in his place. But under the circumstances, that couldn't be helped.

"Hail them," the captain told Paxton.

"Aye, sir," came the com officer's reply.

As Picard watched, the Balduk vessel unleashed another bright red barrage. This time, Idun managed to skew the *Stargazer* past the worst of it, but the ship still shuddered miserably with the impact.

"Sir?" someone said.

The captain saw that Kastiigan had shown up at his side. "Yes, Lieutenant?"

"If you have a dangerous, perhaps life-threatening assignment in mind at this time...I just wanted you to know that I'm ready to embark on it."

Picard nodded, recalling what Ben Zoma and Wu had told him of the Kandilkari's eagerness to place his life in jeopardy. "I assure you, I will consider you before anyone else."

Kastiigan smiled. "Thank you, sir." And he returned to his science station.

"Mr. Paxton?" Picard prompted.

The com officer shook his head. "Nothing, sir. They're not responding."

Again, the Balduk ship stabbed at them with directed energy fire. And again, Idun managed to keep the ship from taking too much of a beating.

"Try again," said the captain.

Paxton bent to the task. But after a few seconds, he had to make the same report as before. "No response."

Suddenly, the Balduk vessel took a desperate chance for a combatant in so comfortable a position. Instead of continuing to harry the *Stargazer* from a distance, she put on a blinding burst of speed and fired her phasers at point-blank range.

Picard swore...and braced himself.

Gerda Idun watched her counterparts take off down the corridor, their haste a response to the urgency in Captain Picard's tone.

And they weren't the only ones. Refsland and his companions had taken off as well, albeit in the opposite direction. Though they weren't required to appear on the bridge, they had their own stations to worry about.

Before she knew it, she was on the move as well, pulled along by Lieutenant Joseph. "Let's go!" he told her.

"Where?" Gerda Idun asked, following him down one corridor and then another.

"To security," he told her. "It's not far from here."

She didn't have to ask Joseph why he needed to go there. As acting head of that section, he would be charged with directing any emergency procedures.

Gerda Idun wondered what he would do with *her*. After all, security was a strategically sensitive location, and her chaperone had studiously kept her away from such places.

But more than that, she wondered about Gerda. Though the navigator's feelings about Refsland had obviously been building for some time, her behavior had been inexcusable—at least, by Gerda Idun's standards.

And the way Gerda had left the gym after her sister sparred with Gerda Idun...that was strange as well. Was she always so volatile? And if so, why wasn't Idun like that?

Before she could venture an answer, something happened—something big and bright and much too loud, as if a thousand people were shrieking all at once.

Then it stopped. *Everything* stopped. And somehow, an impossibly long time later, it started again.

Propping herself up on an elbow, Gerda Idun opened her eyes. Her ears were ringing, her head felt like it was stuffed solid with cotton, and she felt pain when she tried to move—*lots* of it.

Yet a moment's inspection told her she was still intact. It was more than she could say for her surroundings.

Looking around her, Gerda Idun saw a corridor swiftly filling with smoke, and a spray of sparks coming from one of the bulkheads. Obviously, the aliens had scored a direct hit on the *Stargazer*—maybe even breached the hull.

I have to find a more secure part of the ship, she told herself. If the aliens pounded away again at the same place, she would be a goner.

Gerda Idun had already taken several steps down the corridor when she remembered that she wasn't alone. *Joseph,* she thought. *Where was he?*

She scanned the corridor in both directions, but couldn't find any sign of him in all the fumes. Had the security officer already gotten out of there on his own?

No, she insisted silently. Not if he was anything like the Pug Joseph in *her* universe. More likely, he was lying on the deck somewhere, injured—or worse.

With that in mind, Gerda Idun started searching for him, waving her arms as she waded through the increasing billows of smoke. She found herself gagging on the stuff, but there was no way to avoid it—not if she wanted to find the security officer.

Damn, she thought. The corridor was only so big, and the blast could have carried him only so far. Where could he be?

Her eyes burning, she made her way back and forth from bulkhead to bulkhead, methodically covering as much ground as she could. If Joseph was there, she told herself, she would eventually stumble over him.

But it was rapidly becoming harder for Gerda Idun to breathe. Her throat and chest already felt like they were on fire, and it was only going to get worse. She estimated that she had another thirty seconds—no more—before she succumbed to the smoke and lost consciousness.

It didn't matter. She couldn't leave without Joseph.

Suddenly, she caught a glimpse of something red and black and low to the floor. But it was only for a moment. Then the smoke roiled over it.

Darting in that direction, Gerda Idun found what she was looking for—the prone form of a man in uniform. Turning him faceup, she saw that it was Joseph, all right.

But he wasn't moving, and his temple was awash with blood. Not good, she thought, hauling him up and dragging his arm across her shoulders. Not good at all.

Struggling with the burden of Joseph's deadweight, Gerda Idun lowered her head and plowed along the corridor, praying that she would find breatheable air before she passed out and doomed the two of them.

Picard pulled himself back into his center seat and regarded the Balduk vessel on his viewscreen.

Idun had managed to maneuver them off the enemy's bull's-eye. But the Balduk commander had gotten a telling shot in, hammering the *Stargazer* at close range.

As someone rushed to put out a sparking, flaming aft console, Picard turned to Gerda. "Damage report!"

"Shields down fifty-eight percent!" she told him. "Hull breaches on Decks Eight and Nine!"

He bit his lip. It was too soon to know about casualties, but he was sure there would be some of those as well.

Picard eyed the viewscreen again. He didn't like being run off by those who had no more claim to this area than he did. However, he wasn't going to further endanger his ship and crew without a compelling reason to do so.

Turning to Idun, he said, "Take us out of here, Lieutenant. Full impulse."

His helm officer, who had the heart of a Klingon warrior, had to like the idea of retreat even less than he did. However, she followed his orders without hesitation, bringing the *Stargazer* about and withdrawing at the speed the captain had indicated.

Picard shook his head as he watched the Balduk ship diminish on his viewscreen. His adversaries weren't making even a token effort at pursuit. But then, why should they? By their lights, they had accomplished their objective. They had driven off the Federation invader.

At least, he added silently, *for now.*

Ejanix frowned as he returned to the storage room that Kovajo was using as an interrogation facility.

It disappointed him greatly that he couldn't make Vigo see the need for rebellion. But then, as he himself had pointed out, the weapons officer had been born into an Elevated Caste. He hadn't witnessed what Ejanix had witnessed.

And on top of that, he had been steeped in Starfleet philosophy. Ejanix had only been an instructor, not a cadet. It was easier for him to break the habit.

Still, the engineer couldn't help feeling he might have swayed his old friend if he had been more eloquent—if he had painted pictures with his words the way Kovajo and some of the other rebels did.

But rhetoric had never been Ejanix's strength, and politics had always seemed as distant to him as the stars. So it was difficult for him to convey what others had so aptly conveyed to him—the misery, the injustice, and the despair of living a Lesser Caste life.

He would have known of the situation firsthand, but for the government's desire to nurture his superior intellect. Ever since he could remember, both he and his family had been insulated from the life of the Lesser Caste.

It took a friend, who introduced him to Kovajo and some of the other rebels, to make him see the truth.

After that, he would never look at his homeworld the same way.

Ejanix sighed. Perhaps it been foolish of him to think he could open Vigo's eyes.

Once, he and Vigo had been friends. They had agreed on most everything. But under the circumstances, it was doubtful they would agree on anything ever again.

There was a rebel outside the interrogation room, a phaser in his hand and a suspicious expression on his face. But then, Kovajo was the only rebel who had met Ejanix prior to this venture. It was only natural that everyone trusted him less than they trusted each other.

Ejanix nodded to the man. Then he went inside.

Kovajo and a couple of the others had pulled chairs into the center of the room and were talking about something in harsh whispers. When they saw Ejanix, they fell silent.

"I spoke to Vigo," he said. "But I didn't get very far."

Kovajo made a face, then glanced at the others. "Too bad. We need to get that shuttle back in the air."

The way he said it, it wasn't just a goal. It was an absolute necessity, to be achieved at any cost.

"And we need to do it quickly," he added, "before someone in the Federation realizes what we're up to."

"But Vigo won't tell us what he did," said Ferrak, Kovajo's second-in-command, "and neither will the other weapons officers—if they even know."

"Then we'll have to make our interrogations a little more productive," said Kovajo.

"They're Starfleet," Ferrak noted. "Sometimes they die before they crack."

Kovajo considered that. "All right," he said. "We've got a number of engineers in hand, haven't we? If the weapons officers won't help us for their own sakes, maybe they'll do it for the flower of Federation genius."

Ferrak nodded. So did the others.

But Ejanix wasn't nodding. Kovajo speared him with a glance. "You disagree?"

Ejanix saw the look in Kovajo's eyes—a significantly more feral and dangerous look than when they first took over the installation—and shook his head.

"No," he assured the other Pandrilite. "I was just...thinking."

Kovajo tilted his head. "About what?"

"A better way," said the engineer. "One that doesn't require us to inflict any more pain."

"If I didn't know better," Kovajo replied slowly and thoughtfully, "I would think you're putting your friend's welfare ahead of our cause."

Ejanix shook his head. "I'm not, believe me. I'm just—"

"Good," said Kovajo. "Then we're all of one mind." He glanced at Ferrak. "Grab one of the engineers and bring him to the weapons officers' room. I'll meet you there."

Ferrak nodded. "Done." Gesturing for one of the other rebels to follow him, he left the room.

Kovajo eyed Ejanix, as if to gauge his reaction. But the engineer remained silent. He was afraid that if he protested again, he might end up under guard himself.

He recalled something Vigo had said to him, his face

battered and bruised. *Take a good look, Ejanix. Is this justice?*

It's regrettable, the engineer told himself. *Highly regrettable. But if we don't get off this world, our cause may be forfeit.*

What was the pain of a few colleagues compared with the prospect of true justice on Pandril? He could live with it if it brought them victory in the end.

Yes, he thought, *I can countenance a little more blood, a little more suffering.*

Or so Ejanix insisted to himself. But it took an effort for him to make himself believe it.

Vigo looked up when he heard the sound of approaching footsteps. This time, he could tell from their cadence that it wasn't Ejanix who was making them.

A moment later, he saw Kovajo and one of the other Pandrilites join the guards at the entrance. It didn't bode well for the weapons officers.

"There's your pal," said Sebring, "back for another go-around."

"Vigo!" Kovajo called out.

The *Stargazer* officer got up and went over to the transparent barrier. Only then did he see that someone other than the rebels was standing in the corridor.

Riyyen was there too.

He looked pale, even for a Dedderac. But he didn't plead with his captors. He just stood there, as stoic as any Pandrilite observing the Third Virtue.

Kovajo grabbed Riyyen by the front of his tunic.

"You see him?" he asked Vigo. "Take a good look. The next time, he won't be standing on his own."

Vigo's teeth ground together. "Why?" he asked. "He doesn't know anything about your shuttle."

"But *you* do," said Kovajo. "And if you don't tell me how to fix it, your friend here will have to pay the price."

Vigo didn't want to put the engineer in jeopardy. But he couldn't give the rebels the information they needed—no matter what price they exacted.

"All right," said Kovajo. "Have it your way." He twisted the front of Riyyen's tunic in his fist. "I just hope I don't get carried away and do something foolish."

Then he pushed the Dedderac down the hallway and followed him out of sight, leaving Vigo and his comrades to think about what he had said.

"I wish they would let this barrier down," said Sebring, "just for a second or two. I would make *certain* a few of them got carried away."

Vigo didn't say so, but he felt much the same way.

Chapter Thirteen

PICARD LOOKED DOWN at Gerda Idun. She was lying on one of Greyhorse's biobeds, her face a mask of soot streaked with threads of perspiration.

He turned to his chief medical officer, who was standing beside him. "Will she be all right?"

"She'll be fine," Greyhorse told him. He jerked a thumb over his shoulder. "And so will Joseph, thanks to her pulling him out of that corridor in time."

"Yes," said Picard. "I heard."

Not so long ago, he had looked at Gerda Idun with a healthy amount of suspicion. It was a lot more difficult to do so now, after she had saved the life of the man who was supposed to be watching her.

Had she been up to no good, she had certainly had her chance to demonstrate it. With the ship in a state of battle alert and her escort unconscious, she could have accessed any of several systems and done all kinds of damage.

Instead, she had rescued Picard's security chief. And judging from the reports he had received, she had done it at great risk to her own life.

If Gerda Idun had been one of his officers, he would have placed a commendation in her file. As it was, all he could do was thank her.

"Would it be a problem to wake her up?" the captain asked Greyhorse.

The doctor produced a hypospray. "Actually, I was about to do that anyway." Pressing the device against Gerda Idun's arm, he released its contents into her system.

A moment later, her eyelids fluttered open and she looked around. "Pug—?" she groaned.

"He's all right," said Picard.

"Thanks to you," Greyhorse added.

The captain noted the look on the doctor's face as he regarded Gerda Idun. Clearly, Greyhorse admired what the woman had done—and he was a hard man to impress.

Their guest took a deep breath and let it out again. Her brow wrinkled. "No pain."

"Your lungs took a beating," the doctor told her, "but I was able to prevent any serious damage. You may have some discomfort when the painkillers wear off, but nothing you won't be able to handle."

"Thanks," she said.

Picard knew two things.

One was that Gerda Idun had earned a good deal more freedom. He would no longer insist on having her escorted about the ship. A combadge that would let him keep track of her whereabouts would suffice.

The other thing was that he would get her back to her own universe, Balduk or no Balduk.

Nikolas breathed a long, heartfelt sigh of relief as he stood at Vigo's weapons console.

When he heard that Gerda Idun had been hurt, that she had been taken to sickbay, he had gone numb all over. It was almost as if *he* were the one who had been stricken by potentially lethal EPS explosions.

In fact, it had taken all of his willpower to keep from bolting for the turbolift and going down to sickbay to see her for himself.

Then, just a moment ago, he had heard the good news—that both Gerda Idun and Joseph would be all right. That, in fact, Gerda Idun had gotten the security officer out of the danger zone all by herself.

Hence, the sigh of relief.

Obal couldn't have been more wrong, Nikolas told himself. This wasn't just a physical attraction. The ensign had never felt this way about anyone before.

And just his luck, the object of his affection was determined to leave him. In fact, she was determined to leave his whole damned universe.

Nikolas didn't know if he could handle that. If there were only another way...

Suddenly, it came to him. There *was* another way. And when he saw Gerda Idun, he would tell her about it.

* * *

Wutor was still basking in the glow of his victory over the Federation starship when Delakan called to him from her data-collection panel.

"We're being prodded by another ship," she said, studying her monitor. "The *Asajanarin*." She looked up, an expression of disgust on her face. "A High Order vessel. With a full seven subordinates in tow."

The commander nodded. "I'll talk with them."

A moment later, his viewscreen filled with the image of another Balduk, his tongue sliding confidently over his teeth. "I am Ujawekwit, commander of this vessel."

Wutor could tell from Ujawekwit's bearing and accent that he was an aristocrat, an individual from a family with ample lands—just like Wutor's own family, prior to his blunder. No doubt, he was used to being obeyed.

"And I am Wutor," he spat back. "What do you want?"

The commander of the *Asajanarin* smiled, his lips pulling back from his teeth. "You may depart now," he said with High Order disdain. "I and my subordinates will see to it that this portion of Balduk space remains inviolate."

Wutor had expected this sort of behavior. In fact, he would have been shocked if his High Order counterpart had taken any other approach.

"I have no intention of departing," he snarled. "The *Ekhonarid* has already clashed with the invader and repelled her. According to Law, these coordinates are mine to guard and defend." He leaned forward in his brace. "Though you may stay here and assist me, if you like."

The High Order commander's eyes narrowed beneath

his brow ledge. "I do not assist Middle Order vessels. Stand aside and I will forget your insult."

It was a game, just like the one Wutor played with Tsioveth. Ujawekwit knew only too well that Wutor was within his rights. He was just hoping he could intimidate him into giving them up.

But Wutor had been fortunate to stumble onto such an exquisite opportunity, and he might never stumble upon another one. He wasn't about to relinquish it so easily.

"The defense is mine!" the commander of the *Asajanarin* insisted angrily.

"It belongs to *me!*" Wutor barked back. "You know the protocols. Or do you wish to poach on my coordinates and risk the wrath of your overseers?"

Ujawekwit couldn't take that chance, and they both knew it. If his overseers found that he had knowingly violated the protocols, he might be stripped of his command—and perhaps a portion of his lands as well.

"Well?" Wutor prodded.

The other commander glared at him. "I will stay," he said, each word cutting like a dagger, "and assist you in your defense of Balduk space."

It was clearly the wisest course of action for all concerned. "Good," said Wutor, providing the ritual response as he settled back comfortably into his brace, his position secured. "I welcome your assistance."

Gerda glanced at her sister, who was sitting beside her at the bridge's helm console.

More than an hour had passed since they took their

stations in the midst of the battle with the Balduk. Normally, Idun would have said something to her sister in all that time, or at least cast her a knowing glance. But she had done neither.

Clearly, she wasn't happy with the way Gerda had acted with Lieutenant Refsland earlier. In fact, Gerda wasn't happy with her behavior either. No matter what kind of thoughts the man had entertained, it didn't justify her assaulting him.

But Idun was her *sister.* She wasn't supposed to turn a cold shoulder to Gerda, regardless of the circumstances.

Suddenly, one of the navigator's long-range sensor monitors began flashing. Turning her attention to it, she saw that Gerda Idun's return to her own universe had just grown significantly more complicated.

"Sir," she said, turning to Captain Picard, "sensors are picking up additional Balduk signatures."

Picard looked at her. "How *many* more?"

Gerda consulted her monitor again, then turned back to him. "There are now nine vessels, all told, though all but one is smaller than the first."

The captain got up from his seat and looked over the navigator's shoulder. Seeing the ranks of the opposition for himself, he looked anything but happy.

"Get me what you can on them," he said.

Gerda nodded. "Aye, sir."

She shared his concern. If it had been difficult to get near the anomaly before, it would now be a good deal more so. Clearly, Picard had his work cut out for him.

Gerda glanced at her sister again. It wouldn't do the

Stargazer any good for Idun to start speaking to her, but it would certainly make *her* feel a lot better.

Ejanix couldn't hear the sounds Riyyen made as Kovajo's men beat him, because Ejanix had placed himself in a room at the other end of the installation.

But he *imagined* that he could hear them—every last groan and gurgle and unanswered plea for mercy.

How had it come to this? All Ejanix had wanted to do was improve the lives of his people, and perhaps bring a little justice to Pandril. At the outset, it had seemed like such a golden ambition.

But somewhere along the way, the gold veneer had worn off, and the base, dark metal underneath had begun to show through. Ejanix saw now that the rebel movement wasn't quite as pure as he had first believed.

They weren't above resorting to violence—and not just of the kind that put them and their fellow Pandrilites on opposite sides of a phaser battle.

There was a worse kind of violence, Ejanix had realized. And it was going on now in Kovajo's interrogation room, for the sole reason of forcing Vigo to tell them what he knew.

Finally, Ejanix couldn't take it anymore. Bolting from the room in which he had sequestered himself, he made his way down one corridor and then another.

Finally, he came to the interrogation room. The door, he saw, was open. There weren't even any guards outside it.

Sensing that something was wrong, the engineer swung inside—and saw some of the rebels, Kovajo included, gathered in a knot at the center of the room. At first, Ejanix didn't see any sign of Riyyen. Then he realized that the Dedderac was sitting at the center of the knot.

"How did this happen?" Kovajo demanded of Ferrak.

Ferrak held his hands out. "I don't know. I didn't hit him that hard, I swear it."

Ejanix felt his throat constrict. With legs that felt like someone else's, he moved closer to get a better look at Riyyen. The Dedderac's head was tilted back, his mouth was open, and his eyes were staring at the ceiling.

"By the Virtues..." Ejanix said softly.

Riyyen was dead.

Having heard him speak, Kovajo and the others turned to look at him. They looked like children who had gotten caught with their hands full of sweets.

"He was a Dedderac," Ejanix said. "His physiology is different from ours."

He knew then that he should have said something to that effect earlier, but he hadn't. Like Riyyen's murderers, he hadn't expected the differences to be that significant.

But apparently, they were.

Suddenly, Kovajo was in front of Ejanix, cutting off his view of Riyyen. "You can thank your friend for this," he said. "Had Vigo cooperated with us, we would never have resorted to anything of this nature."

Ejanix nodded. "Of course."

But in the shelter of his own mind, he was thinking again of something Vigo had told him. *And will it be a bloodless revolution, Ejanix?*

The engineer swallowed. *What have I done?*

Chapter Fourteen

THE BALDUK WERE REKNOWNED as a savage-looking breed. Their leader was no exception.

He had pitted, pitch-black skin with scars denoting his rank, mere holes for ears, and eyes that were like tiny, pale green fish darting between jutting brow ridges and painfully prominent cheekbones. His thick, white hair was gathered into a cascade at the back of his head, giving him a vulpine appearance, and as he spoke his long, narrow tongue slithered across an abundance of short, sharp teeth.

"I'm here," said the Balduk.

Picard nodded approvingly. It had taken hours of patient work on Paxton's part, but the com officer had finally gotten their adversary to respond.

"I'm Jean-Luc Picard," he said, "captain of the *Stargazer.* Thank you for answering our hails."

The Balduk leader didn't identify himself. He just said, "What do you want?"

"A cessation of hostilities," said the captain. "We need to return—briefly—to the anomaly we were studying and we don't wish to have to fight you for that privilege."

The Balduk's pale green eyes narrowed with suspicion. "Why do you *need* this?"

"Because when we were in the vicinity of the anomaly earlier, we inadvertently took on board a being who doesn't belong in our universe. We believe the only way to send her home is to re-create the conditions that brought her to us—including the proximity of the anomaly."

Picard didn't see any need to mention that the being in question was human, or that she was from a mirror universe, or that Starfleet personnel had had contact with another mirror universe seventy years earlier. He simply laid out the essential facts and waited for a response.

The Balduk's tongue insinuated itself among his teeth. The captain recognized it as an indication that his adversary was considering the situation.

Finally, the Balduk spoke again. *"Home* is important. We understand the being's need to return. But the anomaly, as you call it, is in my people's space."

Picard wanted to tell the fellow that he had a most convenient grasp of stellar geography. But under the circumstances, he bit his tongue.

"I am not disputing your right to that part of space," he said. "I am simply asking for access to the anomaly for a short period of time."

The Balduk's tongue slithered some more. Then he

shook his head from side to side. "If your ship violates our borders, we will destroy it."

"But," Picard argued, "it would not be a violation if you granted us free—"

Before he could finish, the Balduk's image vanished from the viewscreen. The captain found himself talking to a vast, unbroken field of stars.

Not that it mattered. Obviously, he would sooner get help from the unheeding stars than he would from the Balduk.

Nonetheless, he had been right to ask. Had he succeeded in his request, it might have saved lives on both sides.

"You know," said Ben Zoma, leaning close to him, "Simenon is almost ready."

"But it won't do any good," Picard noted in response, "unless we can get near the anomaly."

"So what are you going to do?"

The captain eyed the viewscreen. "Whatever it takes to get Gerda Idun home."

Ben Zoma nodded. "That's what I thought you'd say."

Nikolas touched the metal plate next to Gerda Idun's door and waited for it to slide open. When it did, he smiled at her and said, "Surprise."

She smiled back, though she looked a little weary. "Come on in."

"I looked for you in sickbay," he explained as he entered Gerda Idun's quarters, "but Greyhorse told me he had already released you."

"Yes," she said, depositing herself in a chair on one

side of the room and leaving Nikolas its counterpart on the other side. "I wasn't hurt as bad as I might have been."

He nodded. "I'm glad."

Gerda Idun must have seen something in his eyes then, because her smile faded. "It's sweet of you to check on me," she said, "but I was just about to go to bed. I guess I'm still feeling the effects of the medications the doctor gave me."

"Nonsense," Nikolas told her. "Nobody walks out of sickbay still feeling the effects of medication. You're just trying to get rid of me."

She chuckled—nervously, he thought. "And why would I do that?"

"Because you don't want to hear what I've got to say."

"And that is?"

"That I'm falling in love with you," he told her, the words sounding perfectly natural to him. "And that I want to be with you, in this universe or any other."

Gerda Idun stared at him. "That's…that's very flattering," she said, uncharacteristically caught off guard. "But you don't know what you're saying."

The ensign laughed. "You may be right about that. This probably isn't the most well-thought-out decision I've ever made. But it doesn't matter. I'm determined to spend the rest of my life with you."

"It's impossible," Gerda Idun told him. "You can't go where I'm going."

"We don't know that," he insisted. "If you can be sent back there, maybe I can too."

She shook her head. "We'll be lucky if the circuits

hold together long enough to transport one person. Two would be out of the question."

"Simenon hasn't said that," said Nikolas. "If there's even a chance—"

Suddenly, a tear ran down her cheek.

It was so unexpected, so unlike her, that it drew him to her the way a lump of iron was drawn to a magnet. He crossed the room and joined her on the other side, knelt in front of her and took her hands in his.

"The rest of my life," Nikolas told her.

Gerda Idun shook her head. "No."

He started to protest, but she put her hand over his mouth.

"Not the rest of your life," she said firmly. Then her features softened and she added, "Just tonight."

And she kissed him long and passionately.

Vigo was almost done eating the food he had been given when he saw Runj turn his head toward the corridor—an indication that one of their captors was coming back to see them.

He was surprised when it turned out to be Ejanix.

After their last conversation, Vigo hadn't expected his mentor to return any time soon. And yet, there he was, seemingly back for more.

Crossing the room to where Vigo was sitting, he got down on his haunches again. As the rebels at the door watched with interest, he looked the weapons officer in the eye. "I thought you would want to know...I considered what you said."

The weapons officer looked at him. "And?"

"And nothing's changed. I still feel as I did before—that we're right to do as we do."

Vigo sighed. "It's difficult for me to believe you're the same man I learned from back on Pandril. The Ejanix I knew would never have violated the Virtues by gloating—even if he had something to gloat about, which you don't."

The gibe didn't seem to bother Ejanix. Obviously, he had been prepared for such a remark.

"You may not think what we're doing here is something to be proud of," he said, "but when history judges us, it won't be with an Elevated Caste eye. We'll be judged by those whose lives have been made better by our rebellion."

"By Kovajo," said Vigo, "and others like him."

"I hope so," Ejanix said unflinchingly.

"And the bloodshed that will take place between now and then? What will history say about that?"

"That it was necessary," Ejanix said. "And that in the long run, it prevented more misery than it caused."

Vigo saw there was no point in arguing. Clearly, his mentor had made up his mind.

Ejanix must have realized he wasn't going to get a response, because he got up and turned to go. But he had hardly taken a step when he stopped and turned around again.

"You know," said Ejanix, "I was thinking...how well do you remember Velluto's?"

Vigo regarded him. "The restaurant? In San Francisco?"

Ejanix nodded. "We never ate the food there, did we? They didn't serve anything we could eat. But we liked to sit at the bar and drink grape wine."

"Yes," said the weapons officer, wondering why Velluto's wine list had come to mind at such a bizarre time. "I remember."

"I enjoyed those evenings," said Ejanix. "I remember how much I used to hate it when the manager announced it was closing time. Do you remember that as well, Vigo?"

He did. He said so.

"They closed the same time every night," said Ejanix. "They were very precise about it."

"I remember," Vigo told him.

Ejanix's gaze seemed to sharpen then, to pierce him. "Have a pleasant evening."

It was what the manager at Velluto's used to say as he escorted Vigo and Ejanix to the door. The weapons officer could hear the words in his head.

"Have a pleasant evening, gentlemen. A very pleasant evening."

But why was Ejanix repeating it now? And why was he staring at Vigo so strangely?

"It's unlikely," said Vigo, "that I'll have anything even approaching a pleasant evening."

Ejanix didn't say anything more. He just stared at the weapons officer a moment longer. Then he turned and departed—this time, for real.

The words echoed in Vigo's ears again, recalling that happier place and time. *"Have a pleasant evening…"*

And as Ejanix had said, Velluto's closed the same time every night. At twelve o'clock sharp. There was never any deviation from that standard.

Twelve o'clock. Time to go. *"Have a pleasant—"*

Suddenly, Vigo thought he understood what Ejanix had been telling him.

Of course, he thought, *I may be misinterpreting the situation completely.* Ejanix might not have meant to communicate such a thing at all.

But Vigo's instincts told him that he was right. They told him that Ejanix was trying to say something in words only the two of them would understand.

Of course, there was only one way to find out—and if the weapons officer was correct, the opportunity to do so would present itself soon enough.

Gerda was pacing her room like a caged *targ* when she heard a chime announce the presence of someone at her door.

Greyhorse, she thought.

He had come to try to apologize for what she had seen in him. *But should I accept his apology?* she asked herself. *Or should I let him stew in his own bitter juices?*

Normally, she would have opted for the latter. But without Idun, she needed someone to talk to, and Greyhorse had always been happy to listen to her.

I'll accept it, then. But not easily. With her decision made, she said, "Come in."

The door slid aside. But it wasn't Greyhorse it revealed. It was Idun.

For a moment, they stood there staring at each other. Then Gerda moved to one side and let her sister enter.

As the doors closed behind Idun, she glowered at Gerda. "What is the matter with you?" she asked.

Gerda glared back at her with equal intensity. "I might ask you the same question."

Idun looked as if she had expected a different reaction. "Perhaps my memory is faulty—but as I recall, I'm not the one who turned her back on her sister and left the gym without an explanation. And I'm also not the one who attacked Refsland in the corridor."

"Nor are you the one who sees Gerda Idun for what she is," the navigator shot back.

Idun looked more confused than angry. "What in the name of Kahless are you talking about?"

"She's lying about something," Gerda said. "I have seen it in her eyes. She's keeping something from us."

Idun shook her head. "You're insane. All Gerda Idun has done since she came aboard is cooperate with every request the captain has made of her. And if not for her courage, Joseph would likely be dead."

Gerda had to concede that the woman had saved the security officer's life. But that didn't change what she had seen—what her instincts told her was true.

Idun poked her in the small of her shoulder. "I never thought I would be saying this, but you're jealous of her."

Gerda knocked her sister's hand aside with a snap of her wrist. "The hell I am."

"Admit it," Idun pressed. "You didn't see anything in her eyes. You just don't like her being around. Because of the competition she represents. Because instead of two of us, there are three."

Gerda felt a surge of resentment. "Are you calling me a liar?"

"You *are* a liar," her sister told her, her voice growing

husky with anger. "And it's not just me you're lying to. If you think Gerda Idun is concealing something from us, you're lying to yourself as well."

"How can you be certain?" Gerda demanded. "Do you really believe she just appeared on our transporter platform? That it was an accident, as she claims?"

"It happened once," said Idun, her eyes narrowing. "It could have happened again."

"Now who's lying to herself?" Gerda snapped. "Me... or *you?*"

"You have no proof," Idun spat, "no evidence to support your claim. And yet you defame her!"

"And you defend her," Gerda snarled, her face turning hot with fury, "like a blind she-*targ* suckling a rodent!"

Idun looked at her sister with unconcealed disgust. "Our father," she rasped, her voice like a knife, "would have been ashamed to call you daughter!"

It was the worst thing she could have said.

For a long time, as they struggled to survive in an alien culture, the only reward they could embrace was their father's approval. To be unworthy of it was to be worthless altogether—and Idun knew that.

Gerda's wrath carried her like an inexorable, black riptide. *"Pahtk!"* she growled, fully intending it as a challenge, a call to battle.

And for a moment, it looked like Idun would accept it. Her face darkened and her hands balled into fists, as if she would strike her sister like any other enemy.

And Gerda was ready for the blow, if it came.

But it never happened. Little by little, the fire of anger

left Idun's face. Her hands opened and she drew a long, shuddering breath.

Then, with a last look of reproach, she turned her back on her sister and left.

The doors to Gerda's anteroom remained open long enough for the navigator to hear Idun's retreating footsteps. When they hissed closed, Gerda was left feeling emptier than she had ever felt in her life.

Chapter Fifteen

GREYHORSE WAS JUST LEAVING sickbay for his quarters when he saw Gerda in the corridor up ahead of him.

She was wearing a formfitting, gray and scarlet gym ensemble, an outfit she hadn't worn in quite some time—though the doctor didn't know why, considering how good it looked on her.

He hadn't seen Gerda since she stormed out of his office the day before. Normally, one of the things he liked best about sickbay was that he didn't have to interact with people very often. But in this case, it had prevented him from putting his love life in order.

Greyhorse resolved to rectify the situation now, while he still had the chance.

Loping down the corridor to catch up with Gerda, he made sure there was no one else around. Then he caught her by the arm and spun her around, knowing how much she liked it when he acted like a Klingon warrior.

"I want you to listen to me," he said.

Gerda stared at him, obviously surprised that he was behaving so aggressively.

"You were wrong about me," Greyhorse said with an intensity even *he* hadn't expected. "I've never even thought about her."

She didn't know what to say.

"I mean it," he told her. "Not even once. You're the only one I want to be with. The only one—"

Gerda held up her hand. "Doctor," she said, "I've got a feeling I'm not who you think I am."

Only then did Greyhorse realize that he had made a horrible mistake.

Gerda Idun looked up at Greyhorse and saw his features contort into a mask of embarrassment.

"S-sorry," he stammered, "I thought you—"

"Doctor," she said, "please—"

But he continued to sputter. "That is, I—"

"It's all *right*," Gerda Idun said as firmly as she could. "I'm fine. No harm done."

"Yes," said the doctor, still looking a little off balance. "Yes, of course. But you're sure you're not—?"

"Not at all," she insisted. "Really."

He nodded. "Good. Very good. Then I'll...see you around, I suppose."

"I suppose," she said.

A moment later, Greyhorse was moving down the hall with long, purposeful strides, putting the situation behind him as quickly as he could. She watched until he disappeared around a bend in the corridor. Then she smiled.

Obviously, she had stumbled onto something the doctor didn't want her to know about. In fact, if the look on his face was any indication, he didn't want *anyone* to know about it.

Except the person for whom his affection had been intended—either Gerda or Idun, apparently. There was no way at this point to know which one.

Of course, Gerda Idun could have investigated the matter further, and she had to admit to a certain curiosity about it. However, the doctor had been kind to her, and it was none of her business with whom her counterparts carried on their love affairs.

Even if their choice wasn't exactly the one Gerda Idun would have made. She shook her head, bemused.

Of all people... *Greyhorse?*

Picard looked around the briefing room table at his command staff—minus Vigo, of course, and Simenon, who was working on reconfiguring one of the transporter systems. But Joseph was present, having recovered almost completely from his injuries.

"As you know," the captain said, "we have been unable to reason with the Balduk—in part, perhaps, because they now outnumber us nine to one. Nonetheless, I have made a commitment to get Gerda Idun home and I intend to fulfill it."

No one balked at his stance. But then, he hadn't expected them to do so. To the best of his knowledge, everyone liked and respected Gerda Idun—Joseph in particular.

"But," he said, "I cannot do that without gaining access to the anomaly. Therefore, we must devise a method of getting past the Balduk without allowing the *Stargazer* to be destroyed in the process."

Kastiigan raised his hand. "Before we get to that," he said, "there's something I should point out."

Picard looked at him. "Go ahead, Lieutenant."

The science officer reached for the hologram projector in the center of the table and tapped a command into it. A moment later, a three-dimensional representation of the anomaly appeared in their midst.

But it didn't look as it had on the forward viewscreen. It was fuzzy at the edges, indistinct.

"The problem," said Kastiigan, "is not the quality of the image. It's the anomaly itself."

"It's losing integrity," Wu observed.

"That it is," said the science officer. "And at a most unfortunate pace."

Picard swore beneath his breath. "How long will it remain viable?"

Kastiigan shrugged. "Four or five hours, perhaps. But that's just a guess, sir. It could be a good deal less."

And without the anomaly to work with, Simenon couldn't transport Gerda Idun back to her proper universe. Picard tapped his communicator badge.

"Mr. Simenon?" he said.

"Simenon here," came the response.

"How far are you from finishing your work on the transporter mechanism?"

The engineer made a sound of disgust. "Not as soon as I'd like. Another few hours, at least."

"You will have to expedite that," the captain said. Then he told him why.

"I'll see what I can do," Simenon said, clearly not happy about the new wrinkle in the situation.

Picard regarded his officers again, the image of the anomaly looming over them like a sword of Damocles.

"We still need a way to penetrate the Balduk formation," he said, "or it won't matter *how* quickly Mr. Simenon prepares his transporter system."

Idun, Joseph, and Wu all came up with suggestions, but none of them seemed to the captain to have a reasonable chance of success. Then, just when the idea mill seemed to have ground to a halt, Paxton made an observation about the Balduk's vessels.

It was the sort of thing only a com officer would have noticed. Normally, that didn't constitute the basis for a promising combat strategy—but Picard believed this case might be an exception.

He glanced at Ben Zoma. "What do you think, Number One?"

The first officer shrugged. "I think Paxton may have something there. But let's collect some more data to make sure we're not jumping to conclusions."

"I'll get to work on it," Paxton promised.

And with that, the meeting was adjourned.

But on Kastiigan's way out, he paused to speak with the captain. "Sir," he said, "if there is a point in our encounter with the Balduk when you feel the need to imperil me, please don't hesitate to do so."

Picard smiled. "Not for a moment."

The science officer inclined his head and said, "Thank you, sir. I am most grateful."

Then he departed as well, leaving Picard alone in the room to consider the deteriorating anomaly and their chances of reaching it in time.

Vigo checked the digital chronometer on the cargo room wall. It told him that it was precisely two minutes before midnight.

If he were at Velluto's in San Francisco, the manager would be telling him that it was closing time. *Have a pleasant evening, gentlemen. Have a very pleasant evening.*

Time to leave, the weapons officer reflected. Time to take one's friends and go elsewhere.

With a prolonged groan, he got to his feet and stretched—and saw his guards' heads turn vigilantly in his direction. Sebring and Runj had noticed him too, but neither of them seemed to think anything of it.

And why should they? One or another of them had been standing up or sitting down every few minutes since they found themselves imprisoned. It hadn't meant anything before. Why would it mean something now?

Why indeed, Vigo thought.

He walked across the room as if for exercise, passing close by the transparent barrier and the rebels outside it. But he didn't look at them. Why should he?

He was working out the kinks in his legs. He wasn't up to anything trickier than that. Just working out the kinks.

When he reached the far wall, he turned around and

walked back the other way. This time, when he peeked at the guards out of the corner of his eye, they took less interest in him.

No surprise there. After all, he was just walking around. It was understandable that someone forced to stay in a room would want to walk around now and then.

But as soon as he was past the entrance, he glanced at the wall chronometer again. It indicated that it was now twenty-eight seconds to midnight.

If Sebring and Runj had guessed what he was up to, they were hiding it exceptionally well. Neither of them seemed to be taking any particular note of their Pandrilite colleague. They weren't even talking. They were just sitting there, their gazes fixed on something only they could see.

Vigo forced himself to walk all the way to the wall again. Then he turned around and headed back the other way, as if he wasn't quite satisfied yet.

If they were in Velluto's, the manager would be ushering them out the door. *Have a pleasant evening, gentlemen.*

Now that it was Vigo's third pass, the guards were showing even less interest than before. *That was good,* he told himself. Because if he was right, he didn't want them any more interested than they had to be.

He consulted the chronometer. It was only a couple of seconds until the stroke of midnight.

Time, he thought.

And a moment later, the transparent barrier separating him from the corridor fizzled out.

Before either guard could react, Vigo hurtled into

them, slamming them into the wall behind them with bone-jarring force. Then he struck one of them square in the face with all his strength, driving him sideways to the floor.

When he whirled to face the other one, he saw that Sebring and Runj hadn't been as oblivious as they seemed. They were pounding away at the other guard with short, vicious blows, making sure he didn't have a chance to use his weapon on them.

A moment later, he slumped to the floor beside his comrade, a trickle of blue blood issuing from his nose. Neither of the rebels looked like he would wake up anytime soon.

And their phaser pistols lay on the floor beside them, freed from their senseless hands. Vigo snatched one up and Runj secured the other.

"Good work," whispered Sebring, massaging his knuckles. "But how did you know the barrier was going down?"

"We've got a friend in Ejanix," the Pandrilite whispered back, though he still wasn't sure why his mentor had reversed his position.

Sebring smiled. "That guy changes sides more often than I change my uniform."

"What now?" asked Runj.

"We free the others," Vigo told him, and started down the corridor toward the heart of the installation.

But he hadn't gotten far before he glanced back at their guards and thought, *Have a pleasant evening, gentlemen.*

One day, Picard promised himself, he would have a spacious shipboard office with room for mementos and decorations—maybe even a couch for visitors. But for now, he would make do with his ready room on the *Stargazer.*

Sitting in front of his monitor, he studied the data that his com officer had assembled for him over the last half hour or so. Then he turned and looked over his shoulders at Ben Zoma and Wu, who were hovering over him.

"It seems Paxton was correct," the captain said. "Our Balduk friends do appear to exhibit some rather interesting communications patterns."

More specifically, the largest of the nine enemy ships—the vessel Picard had taken to calling the "Coordinator"—had transmitted instructions to the seven smaller ships clustered around her almost constantly.

However, the smaller ships—which he had dubbed "Satellites"—had seldom transmitted any communications of their own. And when they did it was only to acknowledge that they had received the transmissions of the Coordinator.

Furthermore, the Satellites never spoke with each other. They communicated only with the Coordinator.

Then there was the ninth ship—the one the *Stargazer* had intitially clashed with, which Picard now thought of as the "Independent." She communicated with neither the Coordinator nor the Satellites, but kept her own counsel.

"That they do," Ben Zoma agreed. "And if we play our cards right, we may have an opportunity here."

"The only question," said Wu, "is how to exploit it. I suppose the obvious move is to try to jam the Coordinator's messages at a critical juncture, leaving the Satellites without direction."

"Better yet," said Ben Zoma, "let's see if we can feed them some bogus commands."

"And make them our pawns instead of the Coordinator's," said Picard. He nodded, envisioning the possibilities. "Make it so, Number One."

Ben Zoma looked at him. "Make it so...I like the sound of that."

The captain sighed. "If it pleases you, I'll make it a permanent part of my repertoire. Now *go*."

Chapter Sixteen

PICARD WAS REVIEWING their battle plan for perhaps the seventh or eighth time when he heard the sound of chimes. Turning to his ready room door, he said, "Come in."

As the door slid aside, Gerda Idun walked in. She was perturbed by something, if the captain was any judge of such things.

"What can I do for you?" he asked.

"You've been very kind to me," Gerda Idun said. "Kinder than I would ever have imagined."

"It was nothing," Picard said.

She shook her head. "It *wasn't* nothing. You've gone out on a long and very uncertain limb for someone you don't know—and at one time, didn't even trust. But I can't ask you to go out on it any further."

Picard leaned back in his plasticform chair. "What are

you saying? That we need not place ourselves in any more danger for the sake of your transport?"

Gerda Idun nodded. "That's what I'm saying. It's what I *have* to say, if I'm to live with myself."

He regarded her. "That's gallant of you, Lieutenant. And much appreciated. However, you deserve a chance to return home."

She pulled out the chair on the other side of his desk and placed her hands on the polished, black surface. Had anyone entered the room at that moment, they would have thought she was pleading with him for her life.

But it was just the opposite. Gerda Idun was asking him to help her give it up.

"There are a great many people on this ship," she said. "They all have homes to return to just as I do—and people in those homes who will miss them if they fail to come back. I can't ask your entire crew to risk its lives so the needs of a single person can be accommodated."

The captain considered the woman's words for a moment. "It is true," he conceded finally, "that you cannot ask them to assume that risk." He paused. "But I can."

Gerda Idun looked annoyed—a strange thing indeed, under the circumstances. "Why?" she asked. "Because you're their commanding officer?"

"That is correct," said Picard. "But not *just* because I am their commanding officer. I can ask them to do this because they trust me, and because they know I would not ask them to do anything I would not do myself."

Gerda Idun shook her head. "Please, it's not fair to—"

He held up a hand for silence. "It is eminently fair. You talk about not being able to live with yourself. How will my crew feel if they do not at least make an attempt to send you home? How easy will it be for *them* to live with themselves?"

Her nostrils flared. "They don't have any obligation to me. I'm not part of your Starfleet...or your Federation. I'm a stranger to them."

"Perhaps," said Picard. "But can you honestly tell me you would shy away from danger if the tables were reversed—if it were one of my people in your universe, and you had the power to return him or her to us?"

His ready room was never really silent, what with the gentle drone of the engines and the soft whisper of the ventilation system. But it had never been quieter than at that moment.

Gerda Idun sighed. "It's times like these," she said, "when I wish I were a better liar."

The captain smiled. "Rest assured, I would not send my ship and crew on a suicide mission. I sincerely believe we can do this and still emerge in one piece."

She shook her head. "I don't know what to say."

"Say you will speak kindly of us when you return to your proper universe. That will be all the thanks we require." He indicated his monitor with a tilt of his head. "Now, if you will excuse me, we have work to do—*all* of us."

Gerda Idun nodded. "Of course." And without another word, she left the room.

A most remarkable woman, Picard mused. Then he turned back to his monitor and reviewed their battle plan all over again.

* * *

Vigo peered around the bend in the corridor, then pulled his head back and regarded his comrades.

Both Sebring and Runj were eager to strike back at the rebels. They hung on the Pandrilite's words as if they were the riches of some lost civilization.

"Two guards," Vigo mouthed, holding a pair of fingers up for emphasis. "Ten meters away." He pointed to his chest and shook his head from side to side. "They don't know we're coming."

Sebring and Runj nodded to show they understood.

Vigo held his phaser at the ready and counted. "One...two...three!"

Leading the charge down the corridor, he took aim at the nearer of the two guards and skewered him with a bright red beam. As he fell, the other guard realized what was happening and got a shot of his own off.

It scorched the wall to Vigo's right, missing both him and his comrades. Before the rebel could get a second chance, Vigo fired again and sent him sprawling.

That left the room they were watching unguarded. As Runj ran past its entrance to cover them against any other rebels who happened by, Vigo deactivated its transparent barrier.

There were six people inside—the installation's entire complement of security officers. The Pandrilite recognized the woman with the braided black hair who had given Idun clearance to land their shuttle.

Echevarria, he recalled.

"How did you get here?" she asked Vigo.

"Ejanix helped us."

"He's free?" Echevarria asked, her voice a mixture of happiness and surprise.

"Yes" was all Vigo chose to say, since there was no time to tell her the whole story. He jerked a thumb over his shoulder in the direction they had come from. "We were back there. Do you know where they're holding the other engineers?"

She shook her head. "But there are only a few other storage rooms. The engineers are probably in one of them."

Sebring tossed her one of the guards' phasers, keeping the other one for himself. "Let's get going," he said, "before they realize what we're up to."

It was good advice. But with only four phasers among them, it didn't make sense for all of them to go after the engineers.

Echevarria must have come to the same conclusion, because she turned to a Bolian and said, "They might not have found the phaser cache."

The Bolian nodded. "On our way."

Then the two groups split up. The Bolian led the other unarmed security officers in one direction and Echevarria led Vigo, Sebring, and Runj in the other.

But freeing the security people had slowed them down. They would have to move even more quickly now if they were going to stop Kovajo.

Picard was in his quarters, trying to get some much needed sleep, when he was prodded into wakefulness by an insistent and all-too-familiar voice.

"What is it?" he asked finally, propping himself up on an elbow.

"I'm done," said Simenon over the intercom.

"Done?" Picard echoed dully.

"With the transporter system."

The captain winced at the engineer's tone. *Of course,* it seemed to say, *what else would I be done with?*

"You're prepared to send Gerda Idun back?" the captain asked, just to make certain.

"As prepared as I'll ever be," Simenon told him.

Picard absorbed the information. Then he said, "Stand by, Mr. Simenon. Picard out."

Pushing aside his covers, he swung his legs out of bed, planted his bare feet on the room's carpeted floor, and took a deep breath to clear away the cobwebs. Then he looked up at the intercom grid embedded in the ceiling and said, "Picard to Commander Ben Zoma."

"Ben Zoma here," came the reply.

"Mr. Simenon says he's ready to return to the anomaly. Make sure everyone else is. I'll be on the bridge in ten minutes."

"Aye, sir," said Ben Zoma.

Picard padded across the room and got a fresh uniform out of his closet. That way, he could at least *look* rested as he took the *Stargazer* into battle.

From her post at navigation, Gerda saw Ben Zoma look about the bridge at his officers. To her mind, they all seemed ready and alert.

"You heard the man," the first officer told them. "Ten minutes until we head back to the anomaly."

Gerda turned to her sister. As if she sensed the scrutiny, Idun looked back at her.

The odds were stacked against them, the navigator reflected. They were going into battle against forces significantly greater than their own.

If they were to have any chance to succeed, Gerda and her twin would have to work together as they always had—in perfect coordination and harmony. That meant putting their differences aside, no matter how heartfelt they might be.

For the sake of her captain and her crewmates, Gerda had decided to make that sacrifice. She just hadn't known if she was alone in that regard.

But the look in Idun's eye was unequivocal. It told Gerda with ironbound certainty that her sister felt exactly the same way.

Gerda Idun sat down in front of the computer console in her quarters and tried to clear her head. She had anticipated a lot of things when she materialized on this ship, but seeing Andreas Nikolas wasn't one of them.

Of course, it *should* have been. She had fully expected to see counterparts of all her other comrades here, even one of herself. But not Nikolas. After all, he was dead.

But only in her universe. In this one, he was still very much alive, as she had so intimately discovered a mere few hours ago. She found herself smiling yearningly at the thought of it and forced herself to stop.

She and Nikolas couldn't be together. She was going back to her own universe, just as she had told him, and it was impossible for her to take him along. It was that simple.

So why couldn't she stop thinking about him? And why had she spent the night with him, knowing full well it could never happen again?

Because I'm weak, Gerda Idun told herself. But she couldn't afford to be weak any longer. Focusing on the task at hand, she punched a command into her console.

Fortunately, the *Stargazer*'s computer system wasn't very different from the one on her own ship, and what differences existed were easy enough to pick up. She sailed past them, racing unerringly toward her goal....

The crew's level-two personnel files, unrestricted because they didn't contain any sensitive information.

Gerda Idun knew that if she opened them, it would become a matter of record in the ship's data banks. However, she doubted that the notation would raise any eyebrows in the short time she had left here—especially since, as a newcomer to this universe, it was only natural for her to be curious about the *Stargazer*'s crew, and the personnel files were the most logical way to satisfy that curiosity.

Not that Gerda Idun was interested in all the files. Far from it. In point of fact, she was interested in only *one* file. But to cover that up, she opened several others first—starting with Paxton's and then making her way through Joseph's, Greyhorse's, and Kastiigan's.

En route, she learned that Paxton was an expert skier, that Joseph had an allergy to bananas, and that Kastiigan was older than he looked. But none of that mattered to her.

All that mattered, all that she cared about, lay in one file in particular—the one on Phigus Simenon.

Taking a deep breath, Gerda Idun opened it. Then she read through it slowly and carefully, taking the time to scan related links when necessary. Finally, she switched to yet another file—Commander Wu's, as it happened—and left it open while she sat back and considered what she had just learned.

He was Gnalish, just as he appeared. He had graduated from Starfleet Academy with degrees in quantum mechanics, warp field physics, and starship engineering. And his first assignment was on the *Fearless,* an *Excelsior*-class vessel.

Interestingly enough, Simenon hadn't distinguished himself on the *Fearless.* Apparently, he hadn't gotten along very well with some of his colleagues, including his section chief. After less than a year, he wound up on the *Onjata*—a smaller, older, and apparently less prestigious ship.

But it was in the cramped quarters of the *Onjata*'s engine room that Simenon thrived, and was recognized time and again for his insights and ingenuity. As his superiors retired or managed transfers to more prominent vessels, he moved up the chain of command and became the *Onjata*'s chief engineer.

Simenon served in that capacity for six and a half years despite constant overtures from other captains, obviously content to be a big fish in a little sea. Then the *Onjata* was decommissioned, forcing his hand.

He chose to go to the *Stargazer,* a spanking-new *Constellation*-class ship, instead of another old clunker. But he wound up serving with distinction there, first under a man named Ruhalter and later under Captain Picard. And that was all his file said about him.

Funny, Gerda Idun thought. She had expected to see

more superlatives. Complimentary as it was, Simenon's file didn't say he was the most brilliant engineer in the fleet.

And that's what she needed him to be—the brightest, most resourceful, most innovative engineer anywhere around. The top of the line. So much depended on it...

So *very* much.

But she wasn't worried on that count. Joseph had told her what a brilliant fellow Simenon was, and others on the ship seemed to share his opinion.

No, Gerda Idun had been more concerned about quirks that might have turned up in the Gnalish's *medical* history—quirks that might have proven stumbling blocks to her realizing her objective.

But she hadn't discovered any. As far as she could tell, there was nothing to stop her—nothing at all.

Closing Wu's file, she opened yet another one—Lieutenant Chiang's. Then she closed her eyes as she went over what she had to do.

Chapter Seventeen

THIS TIME, Vigo let Echevarria peek around the corner. After all, she knew the place a lot better than he did.

When she pulled her head back back, she told the weapons officers that there were four rebels standing guard outside the storage room. That meant there was something important within, something that needed to be guarded.

It was either the engineers or something equally valuable to the intruders. Prototypes of the tactical devices they had come to steal, perhaps.

In any case, it would be harder to surprise four than two. *This could get messy,* Vigo told himself.

"Hit them hard," Echevarria whispered to them, "and don't stop until you secure that room. Got it?"

The weapons officers all nodded. Then they waited

for Echevarria to make the first move—and went in right after her.

It was messy, all right—but mostly for the rebels. They were standing so close together, they had a difficult time firing back without hitting each other.

Vigo and Runj each cut down an intruder before the others began to return the favor. For a long, tense moment, the corridor was filled with slashing beams of lurid red light. Then another rebel fell, and the last one darted into the room rather than stand alone.

As Echevarria had enjoined them, they pelted down the hall to press their advantage—and it cost them. Three or four beams came slicing out of the doorway at once, forcing them to plaster themselves against the wall to their right.

Of the four of them, only Echevarria didn't move quickly enough. Taking a blast to the shoulder, she flew into the left-hand wall and spilled to the floor. Vigo couldn't tell if she was dead or alive, but her uniform was a smoking ruin where the beam had struck her.

He felt his jaw clench. If they remained where they were, any one of them could be next.

Rather than retreat or wait to be picked off, Vigo did the last thing his adversaries would expect. He ran down the corridor, went into a shoulder roll, and fired into the room.

By the time he came up again, he could see that his maneuver had dropped one of the rebels on the threshold. Better yet, the others had pulled back out of sight, giving Sebring and Runj a chance to advance.

Taking advantage of it, they pelted down the corridor

and launched themselves into the room. Still following Echevarria's advice, Vigo went in after them.

It was another storage chamber, as Echevarria had indicated, but it was a lot bigger than the others and a lot more crowded with heavy metal supply containers. It was also seething with phaser fire, beam after crimson beam searing the air.

Vigo squeezed off a burst as he dove for cover behind the nearest cluster of containers. Then he poked his head out and tried to get a sense of the rebels' positions.

It seemed to him there were at least six of them, probably more. Obviously, they hadn't had any tactical training, because they had allowed themselves to be cut off from the door—their only means of escape.

Also, the rebels seemed to have gathered into two distinct groups—one in each of the room's back corners. That made it easier for Vigo to deal with them.

It also presented him with an opportunity—because there was a tall stack of containers in the back left corner, just behind where the rebels seemed to be hiding.

A directed-energy poke in the right place and that heavy metal stack might be encouraged to topple. And if it did, it would topple on the rebels.

Sebring and Runj, who were hunched behind a collection of containers off to his left, might have seen the possibility too. But it didn't matter. Only Vigo had the angle.

He waited for a respite in the storm of red fury coming from the rebels. Then he raised himself high enough to look over the tops of the containers in front of him, took aim, and fired a beam across the room.

It was answered instantly with another barrage, forcing him to duck again. But Vigo's beam had done its work, knocking one of the lower containers askew.

A moment later, he heard cries of surprise and apprehension as the other containers in the stack came crashing down.

Vigo ventured a look in that direction and saw that it was quiet. No phaser beams stabbing at him, no glimpses of movement. Apparently, his maneuver had worked—leaving only one nest of rebels to contend with.

Then—perhaps out of fear that the weapons officers would try the same thing on them—two other rebels darted from cover and tried to make a break for it.

Vigo fired, but failed to stop them. Fortunately, either Runj or Sebring had better aim, because one of the rebels was knocked off his feet.

But the other one made it through the open doorway. As it happened, he was the most dangerous one, the one they could least afford to overlook.

Kovajo, Vigo thought.

The rebel leader was fast, and he hadn't been battered the way the weapons officer had been battered. But Vigo wasn't about to let that difference deter him.

Swinging out into the corridor, he fired at Kovajo's retreating figure—and missed. But in avoiding the blast, the rebel stumbled and went sprawling.

Certain that he had Kovajo where he wanted him, Vigo extended his weapon and pressed the trigger again. But nothing happened. No narrow red beam, powerful enough to stun the rebel leader unconscious. Not even a spurt of energy.

Nothing.

Either the phaser had malfunctioned or it was out of power—Vigo didn't care which. All he knew was that Sebring and Runj were still exchanging blasts with the rebels in the storage room, and he couldn't let Kovajo get away.

Putting his head down, he charged down the corridor and went flying in Kovajo's direction. The rebel whirled and got a shot off, but all it did was plow a long, black furrow in one of the walls.

Then Vigo was on top of him. But as he landed, Kovajo smashed him in the face with his phaser.

Though it stunned the weapons officer, he couldn't let Kovajo get the upper hand—not while there was still a working phaser in it. Grabbing the rebel's weapon, Vigo tried to twist it out of his grasp.

As they struggled, the phaser went off—and gouged a dark, fuming hole in the ceiling above them. Vigo gritted his teeth as he tried to make sure the next hole wasn't in *him*.

"You can't win," Kovajo told him. "You're soft, just like the rest of your kind."

Determined to prove him wrong, Vigo found some leverage and pried the phaser free. It went skittering down the corridor where neither of them could reach it.

With a cry of rage, Kovajo pulled his fist back and drove it into Vigo's chin, snapping his head back. Then the rebel followed with another blow, and another.

"You're weak," he insisted with a snarl. "Used to getting everything you want."

Then Kovajo struck Vigo again, making the light dance in front of his eyes. The weapons officer struggled desperately not to let consciousness slip away.

The rebel grinned, his face swimming in front of Vigo's. "You've had it good for a long, long time. But that's going to change."

And he cocked his fist to do some more damage. But this time, it didn't have a chance to land—because Vigo reached up and grabbed his tormentor by the throat.

His air supply cut off, Kovajo seized Vigo's wrist and tried to pry it loose. However, the weapons officer had learned a few things about windpipes in his Academy hand-to-hand combat classes, and none of them were good news for Kovajo.

"Damn you—!" the rebel croaked.

You'd like to, Vigo thought.

But he didn't let go.

Kovajo's face darkened by degrees. His eyes looked as if they were trying to pop out of his head. And with every second that passed, Vigo gained more control over his senses.

Finally, the rebel managed to free himself from Vigo's grasp. He sat back and drew in a long, wheezing breath, eager to get air back into his starving lungs.

But by then, the weapons officer was ready for him. With a jerk of his body, he thrust Kovajo off him. Then, scrambling to get his legs underneath him, he hit the rebel as hard as he possibly could.

The Virtues relegated against his taking satisfaction in a victory, no matter how hard fought. But just this once, Vigo ignored the Virtues.

He savored the feeling of his fist plowing into Kovajo's jaw, and the sight of the rebel's head bouncing off the wall behind him, and the sound Kovajo's skull made when it struck the unyielding metal surface.

Just this once, Vigo thought, as he watched Kovajo slump to the floor, unconscious.

"Good for him," someone said.

Vigo turned and saw Ejanix walking toward him. He looked as satisfied as if he had knocked Kovajo out himself.

The weapons officer staggered to his feet and held up his hand for his friend to stay back. "They're still fighting in there," he said, indicating the storage room.

"Not anymore, we're not," said Sebring.

Turning, Vigo saw the human and Runj emerge from the chamber, looking wrung out with the intensity of their effort. But at least they were whole and unharmed.

Vigo retrieved the phaser Kovajo had dropped. Then, together, they went back to see to Echevarria. Fortunately, she was still alive—and would remain so if they got her medical help before too long.

Ejanix wrapped his hand around his friend's arm. "I'm so sorry," he said. "You were right about Kovajo." His eyes screwed up in their sockets. "He killed Riyyen—beat him to death."

Vigo was saddened by the Dedderac's death, but relieved to hear Ejanix's expression of remorse. "It could have been worse," he said, "if you hadn't helped us when you did."

His mentor sighed. "I just wish—"

Whatever he was about to say, it was interrupted by the sound of footsteps. Vigo tracked them to their source—and saw a rebel at the opposite end of the corridor.

No one else had noticed him yet, but the rebel had noticed *them*. In fact, he was aiming his phaser at them, meaning to destroy them.

Vigo was the closest to him. But worn down as he was by Kovajo's blows and sheer weariness, he couldn't move quickly enough to fire first.

All he could do was cry out a warning.

And yet, miraculously, the rebel's beam never reached him—because someone interposed himself between Vigo and his adversary, taking the full brunt of the deadly energy emission.

Then, before the rebel could fire again, he was slammed from the side by another phaser beam. *The security officers,* Vigo thought numbly.

But by then, he was looking down to see who had saved him from certain death—and selflessly forfeited his own life in the process.

No, Vigo thought, as his eyes supplied the answer to his question. *By the Virtues, no...*

It was Ejanix.

Dropping to his knees beside his mentor, Vigo surveyed the terrain of his friend's face. There was dark blue blood bubbling from the corner of the engineer's mouth, a hint of what had to be massive internal injuries—injuries that should rightly have been Vigo's instead.

"Ejanix?" he whispered.

His mentor opened his eyes and saw him. "Yes?" he asked with gentle patience, sounding very much like Vigo's instructor back on Pandril.

The weapons officer shook his head. It didn't seem fair. Ejanix had seen the error of his ways.

The older Pandrilite managed a semblance of a smile. "Imagine," he said, "being killed...by a mere Type-Two phaser. Talk about irony..."

Then he coughed up blood, shuddered, and went limp. And Vigo knew that his friend was dead.

He knelt there on the floor for an indeterminate amount of time, doing his best to understand what had made his mentor change—and then change *back*. And he would have knelt there longer except he felt a hand on his shoulder.

Looking up at the face that went with it, he saw that it belonged to Sebring. The human looked sorry to interrupt.

"The security people say the engineers are okay," Sebring noted, "but some of the rebels are still on the loose."

Vigo nodded and dragged himself to his feet, his weapon still in his hand. "Come on," he said, leaving his friend's remains. "We've got work to do."

Chapter Eighteen

NIKOLAS SAT ON THE EDGE of his bed, knowing full well he was supposed to be on his way to engineering.

Simenon had asked for another pair of hands to help during their imminent battle with the Balduk, and Picard had tapped Nikolas for the assignment. When the captain sent someone somewhere, he expected them to go.

But the ensign couldn't make himself follow Picard's orders. He was too torn apart by the knowledge that once Gerda Idun set foot on Refsland's transporter pad, he would never see her again.

With the morning, Nikolas had grudgingly done what Gerda Idun asked of him—he left her quarters, promising never to come back. At the time, he had deceived himself into thinking he might somehow be able to keep that promise.

But he couldn't. He saw that now with crystal clarity.

Gerda Idun had gotten into him in a way no one else ever had.

It made all the sense in either universe for her to go home alone, and for him to stay where he was. But Nikolas no longer cared what made sense. All he cared about was being with Gerda Idun, now and always.

Planting his elbows on his knees, he ran his fingers through his hair. The captain had told him there might be a promotion in store for him—the kind that might ensure him a future in Starfleet, making fools of all those who had said Nikolas would never make it.

But if he failed to show up in engineering, he could kiss that future good-bye. Hell, he would be lucky if he wasn't court-martialed for insubordination.

No one in his right mind would consider what he was considering—especially for a woman he had met only a few short days ago. No one in his right mind would throw away everything he had worked so hard for and make his way to Refsland's transporter room.

But then, the ensign told himself with a tortured chuckle, no one had ever accused him of being in his right mind.

Picard's forward viewscreen showed him just what he and his crew were up against—the same nine Balduk warships they had detected via sensors.

The Coordinator, a fully outfitted warship bristling with armaments. Its Satellites, considerably smaller but clearly decked out for battle as well. And the Independent, which had already proven herself a match for the *Stargazer*.

A formidable array, to be sure. If anything went wrong, the Federation vessel would be cannon fodder.

But Picard had reviewed his strategy a dozen times. He was confident that it would work.

As for the purple bruise in the flesh of space that was the anomaly...it was diminishing, just as Lieutenant Kastiigan had noted. But it appeared to the captain that there was enough left of it to suit their purposes.

"Picard to Transporter Room One," he said.

"Refsland here," came the reply. "We're all here, sir—myself, Chief Simenon, Chief Joseph, and Lieutenant Asmund."

It made sense for Simenon, who had made the alterations to the transporter system, to be on hand in case anything went wrong. For Joseph, it was just a matter of seeing the woman off.

"In that case," said Picard, "good luck—especially to you, Lieutenant Asmund."

"Thank you," came her reply. "You have my gratitude."

"You're a little premature," the captain told her. "First, let's make sure this works. Picard out."

"Six hundred thousand kilometers," Idun reported.

They were nearing the point at which the Balduk broke off pursuit when they clashed earlier.

Picard glanced at the com station, where Paxton was waiting for the word to do his part.

"Ready?" the captain asked.

Paxton nodded. "Ready, sir."

Picard drew a deep breath and regarded the viewscreen. "Take us in, Idun."

Suddenly, they were slicing into the midst of the

Satellites, headed right for the Coordinator. The Independent tried to get in their way, but it was too late—the *Stargazer* was already surrounded by Satellites.

The captain pointed to his com officer. "Now, Mr. Paxton!"

It was a strange sight to behold—that of his enemies opening a clear and unobstructed path to his objective, when they should have been harrying him with every weapon at their disposal. Yet they were indeed opening a path for the *Stargazer.*

And the commander of the Coordinator had to be more surprised than anyone.

Picard darted a glance at Paris, who was manning the weapons console. "Full spread," he bellowed, "phasers and photon torpedoes!"

Before the Coordinator could maneuver out of harm's way, the *Stargazer* unleashed the spectacular and unrestrained fury of her weaponry. Phased emissions ripped through the Balduk vessel's shields, leaving her naked to the savage force of the matter-antimatter projectiles.

The Coordinator tried to fire back, and a couple of energy volleys found their mark—but the effort was short-lived. In a matter of seconds, the *Stargazer* had reduced her to little more than a hulk floating in space.

Only then did the commanders of the Satellites seem to realize that they had been duped. But without the Coordinator to direct them, they couldn't operate with a single intent.

They converged when they shouldn't have, diverged when it was unnecessary, and even came close to hitting each other with their weapons fire. Paris was able to take advantage of their confusion, picking them off one by one.

And little by little, Idun was able to move them closer to the dwindling anomaly.

Nikolas entered the transporter room expecting to surprise the hell out of everyone present—Gerda Idun included. As it turned out, *he* was the one who was surprised.

Gerda Idun wasn't standing on the transporter pad as the ensign had expected. She was on the other side of the room entirely, fiddling with the transporter controls.

And Refsland, who should have been at the control console, was slumped against the side of it—*unconscious*.

Nikolas didn't get it. In the moment it took him to get his bearings, Gerda Idun snatched up a phaser pistol and leveled it at him.

At that point, he got it even *less*.

"Hey," he said, "it's *me*."

"Stay where you are!" Gerda Idun snapped, her gaze hard and unwavering.

Nikolas shook his head. "What's going on?"

"I'm going home," she told him.

It was only then that Nikolas saw Simenon stretched out on the floor, his motionless form partly concealed by the control console. And it looked like someone else was stretched out alongside him.

The ensign moved sideways to get a better angle and saw that it was Joseph. No doubt, the security chief was where the phaser had come from.

"What did you *do?*" Nikolas asked.

Gerda Idun continued to work the controls with her free hand. "I grabbed Joseph's phaser and stunned him. Then I did the same thing to Refsland and Simenon."

"But why?" he wondered.

She looked up at him, every bit as poker-faced as before. "Because Simenon's coming with me. We *need* him."

Nikolas didn't know what Gerda Idun was talking about, but he knew it wasn't right. "Don't do this," he said.

"I have to," she insisted.

"You can stay here," the ensign said. "With us. With *me.*"

"I can't," she told him. "My people are depending on me to complete my mission."

"Shouldn't Simenon have a say in this?"

Gerda Idun frowned. "Unfortunately, that's not possible."

Nikolas smiled sadly. "I wish like hell it was *me* you needed. I'd go in a second—I think you know that. But I can't let you take Simenon."

For just a moment, her gaze softened and she said, "I didn't think you would." Then she squeezed the trigger on her phaser pistol.

He had been expecting it, so he was able to avoid the full impact of the beam. Still, it spun him around and sent him crashing into the bulkhead.

When Nikolas finally forced his eyes open, the taste of blood thick and metallic in his mouth, he saw Gerda Idun making her way to the transporter platform. And she was pulling Simenon across the deck.

THREE

His body sore and leaden from the punishment it had taken, it was hard for Nikolas to move even his hand. Still, he managed it—and reached for the combadge on his chest.

But it was gone.

Obviously, Gerda Idun had anticipated his using it and taken it away. "Captain Picard," he croaked hoarsely, hoping to access the intercom grid.

"Don't bother," Gerda Idun said as she deposited the Gnalish on the pad. "I've deactivated it."

But she hadn't locked the transporter room doors, the ensign realized, because that required a security override—and she obviously hadn't been able to acquire one.

So there was still a possibility of someone stopping Gerda Idun. But it wouldn't be Nikolas—not anymore.

All too quickly, Picard's combat strategy became a good news–bad news situation.

The good news was that the *Stargazer* was knocking off the Coordinator's Satellites left and right—having already dimmed the lights in four of the seven. The bad news was that as the ranks of the surviving Satellites thinned, it gave the Independent a chance to join the fray.

And it capitalized on that chance by delivering a vicious broadside—one that shook the teeth in the captain's head and poked a hole in a plasma conduit.

Picard did his best to ignore the sudden spurt of superhot gases. "Target the Independent ship and fire!" he called to Paris.

Twin energy beams erupted from their phaser banks and raked the Balduk vessel. But while the Federation ship was occupied with the Independent, the remaining Satellites swooped in and delivered blow after unanswered blow.

"Shields down forty-four percent!" Gerda announced as the deck bucked beneath their feet.

The captain held onto his armrests. So much for getting closer to the anomaly. "Evasive maneuvers!"

Idun took them through a series of dips and twists and ascents, but the Satellites were hard to shake. And every time the *Stargazer* flicked them off with her phasers, the Independent rocked her with another volley.

"Shields down sixty-eight percent!" Gerda reported with a bit more urgency in her voice.

An aft console burst into flame, requiring an officer to douse it with a fire extinguisher.

"Damage to Decks Three, Four, and Five!" said Paxton.

Picard's teeth ground together. Their ploy had worked, but only to a point.

A more cautious commander would likely have withdrawn then and there. But at the rate the anomaly was shrinking, Picard wouldn't get another chance.

It was now or never.

Nikolas bit his lip as he watched Gerda Idun return to the transporter console. He couldn't make himself get up off the floor, but he could still get a few words out.

Was it possible to talk Gerda Idun out of what she was doing? He doubted it. She looked altogether too determined, too committed to her course.

Maybe he could distract her, then. Make her think

about something else. He didn't know what good it would do, but it was better than doing nothing.

"What do you need Simenon for?" Nikolas gasped.

Gerda Idun inspected something on Refsland's transporter console—the sensor monitor, maybe, to check the status of the anomaly. Then she looked up at him, her jaw set, her features devoid of emotion.

"I'm from another universe," she told him, "just as I said. But despite what I told your captain, it's the same universe your Captain Kirk visited years ago."

Nikolas had heard about Kirk's accidental transit at the Academy, and more recently in discussions among his peers. It was a natural topic of conversation when a woman from another universe came aboard.

"In Kirk's time," Gerda Idun continued, "humanity was the oppressor of other species. In my time, it's different. The Klingons and the Cardassians have formed an alliance. Its goal is to wipe us out—every last man, woman, and child.

"They've had us on the run for some time now, but a few of our ships are still putting up a fight. The *Stargazer* is one of them." Her eyes narrowed. "You asked about your counterpart in my universe? Well, he died, all right. But it wasn't when he was in his teens. It was just a few weeks ago, in a battle with a Klingon bird-of-prey."

Nikolas swallowed. He had always known he could die in battle, but it had only been a theory, an abstraction. Suddenly, it was all too real.

"We took other casualties too," Gerda Idun said. "One of them was Simenon. *Our* Simenon."

The ensign was beginning to understand.

"His engineering expertise had been the key to our survival," said Gerda Idun. "One way or another, he had kept us alive through skirmish after bloody skirmish. But the real tragedy is that he was working on a new propulsion technology—something I couldn't even begin to understand—that might have turned the tide of the war in our favor."

Nikolas saw a hint of pain in her face, and a distance in her gaze. It was working. He was distracting her.

And it occurred to him that it might get him somewhere after all—because even though he still hurt like crazy, he felt that he could move his arms and legs a little if he had to.

Keep talking, the ensign thought. *Maybe I'll get another shot at stopping you yet.*

As if in compliance with his silent instruction, Gerda Idun went on. "We had another engineering marvel, a man named Montgomery Scott. In the days of Kirk's Empire, he had served on the *Enterprise* and made a name for himself as a real hardass, but he eventually saw the error of his ways.

"When Simenon was killed, Scott was too old and tired to take over for him. But he was still sharp enough to re-create the circumstances that sent your Kirk from universe to universe—and to use them to transport me here.

"My mission was to cross the transuniversal barrier, find Simenon—either here on the *Stargazer* or elsewhere—and bring him back with me." Her gaze turned hard again. "And that's what I intend to do."

"Despite the kindness the captain showed you," he rasped. "Despite *us.*"

He could see the muscles working in Gerda Idun's jaw. "Yes," she said, without the slightest trace of uncertainty in her voice. "Despite all that."

Chapter Nineteen

IDUN HELD ON to her control console as the *Stargazer* lurched to starboard under a Balduk barrage.

"Shields down seventy-eight percent!" her sister called out from her navigation board.

The air on the bridge was hot and heavy with smoke, there was a metallic reek of leaking EPS coolants, and the lighting faltered every few seconds. But the viewscreen remained in perfect working order, showing them every detail of their enemy's volleys.

Idun could accept the fact that the *Stargazer* was taking a beating. What irked her was that they weren't getting any closer to their goal in the process.

The helm officer was too busy weaving through the enemy's formations to pay attention to her sensor screen, but she knew time was running out on Gerda Idun. If the situation didn't improve—and quickly—the anomaly would vanish and the woman would be stuck in a universe not her own.

Captain Picard seemed to be as determined as anyone to send Gerda Idun home. But even he had his limits, and Idun had a feeling he was about to reach them.

Suddenly, the Balduk pulled a maneuver of which she hadn't thought them capable. Even without the Coordinator to guide them, the Satellite ships pinched the *Stargazer* into the narrowest of escape slots.

Idun drove the ship forward at full impulse. But just when she thought she had slipped their trap, the Independent rose up in front of her.

Blood of Kahless, she thought, the muscles in her temples working furiously.

She tried a roll to starboard—a move that had stood her in good stead before. But not this time. The weapons officer on the Balduk ship tracked the *Stargazer* and buried his phaser beams in her saucer section.

Before Idun could try another tack, the console next to her exploded in a gout of sparks, sending Gerda flying out of her seat. Her heart pounding against her ribs, the helm officer glanced at her sister to make sure she hadn't been killed.

Gerda's hands and face were badly burned, but she was alive. *Alive.* Swearing beneath her breath, Idun turned to her task with a new resolve.

Gerda was the only blood kin she had left in the entire universe. She would be damned if she would let some Balduk marauder take her life.

Diving and twisting to port, she shook the Balduk ship for the moment. Seizing the opportunity, Paris blasted away at the Independent and battered her hindquarters, but not enough to slow her down.

By then, Gerda had gotten to her feet. Even with her injuries, she wanted to stay on the bridge—just as Idun would have, if it had been she who was hurt.

But when the captain ordered her to report to sickbay, she had no choice but to comply. Reluctantly, she limped to the turbolift and disappeared inside it.

Idun felt a pang as her sister departed. But it was only natural for Idun to feel the loss. They were a team.

A team...

She looked at the viewscreen and the enemy vessel depicted there in all her martial glory. Picard had dubbed her the Independent for a reason.

Had the Balduk worked together, they might have driven the *Stargazer* off immediately. But they hadn't. They hadn't even attempted to communicate with each other.

Klingons were warriors too. But they talked. They worked together in a space battle.

Why didn't the Balduk talk? she wondered. *Why?*

It was then that Idun found herself turning to Picard. "Captain," she said, "I have an idea."

It was unorthodox, to say the least. Her father would never have approved of it. But if not for what she had learned from him, she would never have been able to come up with it.

"What is it?" Picard asked, no doubt willing to entertain *any* idea at this point.

"When warriors like these Balduk refuse to talk to each other, it's because they're competing for the right to claim victory—in this case, the victory that would come with driving the *Stargazer* out of Balduk territory."

Picard looked at Idun. "And if that's so?"

"Then we can use it to our advantage." And she told him how.

The captain seemed surprised that she would consider such an approach. After all, she was a warrior herself. But he didn't reject it out of hand.

Finally, he said, "All right. Let's give it a shot."

Idun was gratified that Picard had embraced her suggestion. But she would be a lot more gratified if it got them closer to the anomaly.

Wutor Qiyuntor glowered at his data-collection officer. "What did you say?"

Delakan repeated the message she had received from the Federation ship, this time more slowly and carefully. Still, it was hard for Wutor to believe he had heard correctly.

He turned to his viewscreen, where the *Stargazer* was still veering to one side or the other, trying to shake him from her trail. "I will talk to Picard," he growled.

A moment later, the human's pale, smooth visage appeared on his screen. "Commander," he said, "so nice to hear from you."

"Are you insane?" Wutor demanded.

"Perhaps. Men do strange things in the heat of battle. But for some reason, I feel compelled to surrender to your colleague in the larger vessel."

"You crippled him!" Wutor insisted. "He's no longer a threat to you!"

"Thank you for confirming that," said Picard. "Nonetheless, it's he to whom I'll surrender." His eyes narrowed, as if something had occurred to him. "Unless…"

Wutor leaned forward in his command brace. "Unless what?"

"Unless you give us some time to return our guest to her proper universe."

"Impossible," Wutor spat.

The human shrugged. "The commander of the larger vessel will be pleased to hear that."

Wutor's tongue slid over his flat-teeth. This Picard was cleverer than he would have imagined.

The commander couldn't allow victory to elude him. But if the human surrendered to Ujawekwit, Wutor would emerge from the battle empty-handed—and perhaps remain in the brace of a Middle Order vessel the rest of his life.

On the other hand, he couldn't simply give a Federation vessel an open field in which to squat. He was a Balduk commander. He had a responsibility to guard and defend.

Not to mention a crew who might be inclined to tell tales if he dealt too mercifully with an enemy.

Wutor eyed Picard. "You have fifty heartbeats," he said, "to do what you need to do."

Then, hoping that fifty heartbeats would be enough to resolve all their problems, he broke the line of communication.

Fifty heartbeats will have to do, Picard thought.

"Idun," he said, "get us as close to the anomaly as you can."

"Aye, sir," came the helm officer's reply.

"Captain," said a voice at Picard's shoulder, "I just wanted to take this opportunity to remind you of my availability should the need arise."

Recognizing the tone, the captain darted a glance at its source and said, "Not *now,* Mr. Kastiigan!"

The science officer nodded. "Very well," he replied, and retreated to his station.

Picard looked up at the intercom grid concealed in the ceiling. "Transporter Room One, this is the captain. We're approaching the anomaly. Get ready to—"

"The intercom," said the *Stargazer*'s computer, "is no longer functioning in Transporter Room One."

Picard frowned. "Mr. Refsland, this is the captain."

There was no response.

"Mr. Simenon," said Picard.

Still no answer.

"Mr. Joseph?"

Nothing.

The captain glanced at Ben Zoma, who had moved up from one of the aft stations to join him. "Something's wrong," Picard said, though he couldn't say what it might be.

The first officer seemed to think so too. "Security," he said, "this is Ben Zoma. Get a team over to Transporter Room One on the double."

The captain eyed the Independent, hanging in space with her weapons still trained on the *Stargazer. Fifty heartbeats,* he reflected, *might not be enough after all.*

* * *

Gerda hated the idea of retreating to sickbay. It was true that her hands had been burned and her console had been rendered useless, but she couldn't help feeling there might be something she could do to help.

She was still thinking that when she came across Pierzynski, his long, lean form lying along the left-hand wall of the corridor between the turbolift and sickbay.

The security officer looked up at her, his face badly bruised and one of his legs lying at an awkward angle. Then Gerda saw the reason for it—a still-smoking EPS junction that had exploded a little farther down the corridor.

"I'm all right," Pierzynski gasped.

Judging by the size of his pupils, he had sustained a pretty bad concussion, and his leg was probably broken. But at least he hadn't suffered anything life-threatening.

"Did you call security?" Gerda asked him.

He nodded. "Yes. They're…on their way. But…there are casualties…all over the ship."

The navigator had already decided to stay with Pierzynski until help came when she heard Ben Zoma's voice issue from the security officer's badge.

"Security," the first officer said, "this is Ben Zoma. Get a team over to Transporter Room One on the double."

Transporter Room One was where Gerda Idun would be, along with Simenon, Joseph, and Refsland. It was unlikely that anyone there had been hurt—all the transporter rooms had been overbuilt in order to minimize the possibility of damage.

THREE

So why would the captain have dispatched security there? Gerda had a feeling she knew.

"I've got to go," she told Pierzynski.

Trusting that the security officer would be all right, she made her way back to the turbolift. But this time, she didn't walk.

She ran.

Picard could only guess the duration of a Balduk heartbeat, but he didn't think it would be much different from his own. And his heart had certainly beat more than fifty times since the Balduk granted them a cease-fire.

Come on, Picard thought, silently encouraging his security officers—or, rather, whichever of them arrived in Transporter Room One first. *What's going on down there?*

"Sir," said Paxton, "sensors show an energy buildup in the Balduk ship's weapons arrays."

The captain frowned. Clearly, their reprieve had come to an end. "Evasive maneuvers," he told Idun.

She sent them veering to port just in time to avoid a lurid volley from the Independent. Then, veering back to starboard, she slipped them past a crossfire from the Satellites.

Unfortunately, each maneuver took them a little farther away from the anomaly—and it would be twice as hard to regain whatever ground they lost.

Picard held on to his armrests. Once again, the hunt was on—and the *Stargazer* was more than ever the hunted.

"What's the matter?" Nikolas said, every word an effort.

Gerda Idun frowned as she stood at the transporter console and studied its monitors. "We were almost there."

"Almost at the anomaly," he speculated.

She nodded, still avoiding his gaze. "Yes."

"You know," Nikolas whispered, concealing the fact that his voice was a little stronger now, "I really would have gone back with you."

The muscles around Gerda Idun's mouth tightened, but she didn't say anything.

"I would have left everything," he told her, "to stay with you."

Her nostrils flared.

"Everything," Nikolas said.

Gerda Idun covered her eyes with her free hand, and remained that way for a moment. When she took her hand away, her gaze wandered back to her monitor.

And her eyes, shiny and red as they were with tears, opened wide.

By that sign, Nikolas guessed that Idun had brought them closer to the anomaly again—maybe close enough to effect a transport. He watched Gerda Idun press a stud on the control panel, and hurry across the room to join Simenon on the transporter pad.

If he was going to stop her, he had to do it now, he told himself. Dragging himself along the floor, he worked his way toward Gerda Idun.

Wiping her eyes so she could see better, she trained her phaser on him. "Please," she said, "don't."

Nikolas knew he might not get there quickly enough.

And even if he could, he might not be strong enough to accomplish anything.

Still, he had to try.

Gerda burst into Transporter Room One with unchecked urgency, the doors sliding open for her as quickly as they could.

With a glance, she saw several things. First, that Gerda Idun and Simenon were on the transporter pad, the former standing over the latter. Second, that Ensign Nikolas was dragging himself toward Gerda Idun, hobbled by some injury he must have sustained.

And third, that Gerda Idun had a phaser.

Gerda's hands and face were damaged, but there was nothing wrong with her feet. Picking up speed, she sprinted across the room and leaped into Gerda Idun feetfirst.

But not before Gerda Idun fired her weapon.

Somehow, the phaser beam missed Gerda and struck a bulkhead behind her instead—and that one shot was all Gerda meant to allow. Plowing into Gerda Idun's midsection, she sent the woman sprawling backward. More important, the impact jarred Gerda Idun's phaser out of her hand.

Gerda watched it skitter across the floor and come to a stop. Her every instinct told her to go after it—to get it before Gerda Idun could—and had it not been for Simenon, she would have done exactly that.

However, she doubted that the Gnalish was lying on the transporter platform by accident. Gerda Idun's purpose all along could have been to kidnap

Simenon—though the navigator couldn't begin to say why.

But if it were so, the engineer might be beamed to another universe at any moment.

So instead of going after Gerda Idun's phaser, Gerda scrambled in the direction of the Gnalish. Her scorched hands and face felt as if they were on fire, but she managed to get to Simenon and drag him off the transporter pad.

Then she turned her attention back to the phaser. By then, unfortunately, Gerda Idun had reclaimed it—and was raising it to fire in Gerda's direction.

The navigator didn't even have time to curse. The beam punched her in the stomach and slammed her into the bulkhead behind her, almost knocking her senseless.

When she opened her eyes, she saw Gerda Idun crossing the room, headed for Simenon. As Gerda watched, her counterpart grabbed the engineer by his armpits and dragged him back toward the transporter pad.

"No," the navigator groaned.

Nikolas, who had gotten as far as the middle of the room, raised his arm and pointed to her. "Your badge," he croaked.

Gerda understood. He wanted her to contact the bridge and have them cut power to the transporter.

But that would take time—several seconds, at least. And she could already see the studs on the transporter console lighting up, indicating that a transport was imminent.

Gathering what remained of her resolve, Gerda launched herself at her counterpart. This time, she didn't have the strength for a flying kick. All she could do was drive her shoulder into Gerda Idun's ribs, making her release Simenon and stagger back from the transporter platform.

And before Gerda Idun could strike back, the energizing coils above the pad began to glow.

Gerda knew what that meant. Judging by the expression on Gerda Idun's face, she knew as well.

The transport process had begun. In slightly more than a second, the coils would lock on to whatever matter was directly beneath them and begin breaking it down into its component molecules.

It would be disastrous for any living thing to mount the platform after that point. If Gerda Idun was going to return to her universe, she couldn't delay.

Gerda saw the glint of panic in her counterpart's eyes—the kind of desperation one might see in a cornered animal. Then she watched as Gerda Idun abandoned Simenon, leaped onto the transporter platform, and was bathed in a column of light.

Gerda Idun's eyes were drawn to Nikolas—as if he were the last thing she wished to see in this universe. Then she faded into the light and was gone.

And a moment later, the column of light vanished as well—just as a couple of security officers rushed into the room, their phasers drawn to answer a threat that no longer existed.

Gerda gritted her teeth and forced herself to get up off the floor. As the two security officers went to Nikolas's aid, she touched her combadge with the unburned heel of one hand.

"Captain Picard," she said, "this is Gerda. The transport is complete. We may leave."

"Thank you," said the captain, sounding eminently relieved.

It was nothing, Gerda thought. Then, determined to proceed under her own power, she walked out of the transporter room and headed for sickbay.

Picard didn't know how his injured navigator had wound up in Transporter Room One, but he knew he could rely on the information she gave him.

Turning to his helm officer, he said, "Idun, take us out of here."

"Aye, sir," she returned, executing the command on her control console.

As the drastically shrunken anomaly and the Independent slipped off the viewscreen together in favor of an open starfield, Picard wondered if the Balduk would let them go or take one last shot at them.

He got his answer when Paxton said, "Sir, the Independent is releasing a full spread of photon torpedoes."

Abruptly, the stars ahead of them turned into streaks of light, signifying a jump to warp speed. Picard moved to Idun's seat and gripped the back of her chair.

"Aft view," he commanded.

It showed him that they had left the Balduk behind, but they had yet to outrun the enemy's torpedo barrage.

Picard addressed Idun. "Can we go any faster?"

She glanced at him. "We suffered a great deal of damage, sir. I'm pushing it as it is."

"Push it a little harder," he told her.

"Aye, sir," said the helm officer, and took them up to warp eight.

The captain could feel an unsettling shudder in the deckplates. Still, it was preferable to the jerk of photon-torpedo impacts.

And a moment later, the Balduk's barrage began to diminish as it fell behind them.

Picard heaved a sigh as his first officer moved up to join him. "Well played," said Ben Zoma.

The captain nodded. They had suffered injuries, but none of them fatal. And they had accomplished their objective—they had gotten Gerda Idun home.

Watching the photon flight vanish into the distance, he said, "Mr. Paxton, send a message to the commander of the Independent. Congratulate him on his... victory."

"Aye, sir," said the com officer.

Ben Zoma smiled. "Nice touch."

Picard shrugged. "I would hate to be accused of poor sportsmanship, Number One."

"Captain," said Paxton, "I'm receiving a message from Lieutenant Vigo."

Picard turned to him. *Vigo?* "What does he say?"

"He says he needs help, sir."

The captain didn't understand. What kind of help could someone need on Wayland Prime?

Then Paxton relayed the rest of Vigo's message.

Picard frowned. Given the atmospheric conditions on the installation world, the weapons officer must have been trying for a long time to transmit his call for help.

He turned to Idun. "Wayland Prime, Lieutenant. Best speed."

"Aye, sir," came the helm officer's response as she punched in the coordinates.

Finally, Picard said, "Transporter Room One, this is the captain. Can someone tell me what happened down there?"

It was Joseph who answered. "We had some unforeseen trouble, sir. Gerda Idun wasn't what she seemed."

And he went on to tell Picard what had transpired, including Simenon's role in the affair and Gerda's most timely act of heroism.

"At least," the security chief added, "that's the way Ensign Nikolas described it."

The captain was so taken aback by Gerda Idun's treachery, he didn't even ask what Nikolas was doing there. Obviously, he had misjudged their visitor—misjudged her *badly*.

It made him value the Asmunds of *his* universe that much more.

Chapter Twenty

GREYHORSE LOOKED DOWN at Gerda, her hands and face swaddled in bioplast bandages, the sedative he had administered lulling her to sleep on a biobed.

She seemed so peaceful, he mused. So serene. So different from her waking self.

More like Gerda Idun.

But—despite what thoughts the doctor might have entertained earlier—he had concluded that he didn't want a softer, more human Gerda. He wanted the Gerda he had, boiling to the brim with warrior aggression.

And had she been killed on the bridge instead of merely burned, Greyhorse couldn't imagine how he would have gone on living. He loved her that much.

Reluctantly leaving her side, he moved on to his next patient. Nikolas seemed to be experiencing some discomfort, despite the painkiller the doctor had administered.

"You shouldn't be in pain," Greyhorse told him.

The ensign turned to him, his eyes pleading silently. "I would have gone with her," he said.

The medical officer tilted his head. "I beg your pardon?"

"I would have gone with her, Doc. With everything, I still would have gone."

Greyhorse was about to ask whom Nikolas was talking about. Then he realized he *knew.*

He wished he could have given the ensign some word of consolation, but he wasn't very good at such things. All he could give was his sympathy—because if anyone in the universe knew what Nikolas was feeling, it was Greyhorse.

"Hey," said a rasping voice, "how about a little service down here? What kind of sickbay is this?"

The doctor looked past Nikolas and a few of his other patients, and cast a disapproving eye on Simenon.

"Wait your turn," he said.

Then he left the heartsick Nikolas to take a look at Lieutenant Refsland.

The man known as Scott stood in front of the transporter room's control console, feeling the burden of every year he had survived and every wound he had ever sustained, and helped guide the matter stream into the mechanism's pattern buffer.

After a moment or two, he saw a blinding white column of light. But then, that was how it was with even the most mundane transport, from one room to the next. And this was a lot more than that.

This was a cross-universe event, a breaking down of the barriers between reality and reality. It was the type of thing that wasn't supposed to be even vaguely possible, but somehow *was*.

Scott squinted to see through the brilliance of the effect, but he couldn't. It was too soon to make out the collection of reconstituted molecules inside it, too soon to identify what was slowly but surely materializing.

Come on, he thought. *Ye can do it, lass.*

Finally the column of luminescence started to narrow, to diminish in intensity. And as it did, its contents began to reveal themselves.

Scott could feel his heart pounding. But then, this was a big moment—the sliver of time in which they found out if their struggle had a future or not.

Taking a deep breath, he watched the last of the light fade from the platform. He saw Gerda Idun take shape. And he saw what she had brought back with her.

Scott's jaw clenched. *Nothing,* he thought, eyeing Gerda Idun's empty-handed posture on the transporter platform. She had brought back nothing.

And she was looking wobbly. Weak-kneed, as if she would topple under the weight of her exhaustion.

Biting back his disappointment, Scott came around the console and rushed up onto the platform. Wrapping Gerda Idun in his aged-thinned arms, he made sure she wouldn't fall.

In the process, the engineer caught a glimpse of her face. She was averting her eyes so he couldn't look directly into them, but he didn't have to. Even obliquely, he could see the pain in them, the devastation.

Only then did he understand—it wasn't exhaustion that was making her look so unsteady. It was the knowledge that she had failed in her mission. It was the death of hope.

"I've lost him," Gerda Idun muttered, as if she still couldn't believe it.

"It's all right, lass," Scott told her, knowing even as he said it how hollow it sounded.

It *wasn't* all right. She knew that as well as anyone.

"Scott?" came a voice over the intercom.

It was fuzzy with static, a result of the last pounding they had taken at the hands of the Alliance. Still, the engineer recognized it as the captain's.

Scott looked up and said, "I've got her, Gilaad." He hated the words that had to follow. "She's alone."

The intercom was silent except for a low buzz. Then Ben Zoma said, in a voice that remarkably betrayed none of his despair, "That's too bad."

Scott helped Gerda Idun sit down on the edge of the transporter platform. "We can try it again," he suggested to Ben Zoma.

"No," came the reply. "We can't. They'll be ready for us. They'll know what we're up to."

The engineer sighed. Ben Zoma was right, of course. They'd had one chance, and they'd blown it.

"Ben Zoma out," said the captain with heartbreaking finality, and soon after the buzzing stopped.

Gerda Idun took a tremulous breath and buried her face in her hands. "I've lost him," she repeated.

For the briefest moment, Scott had the eerie feeling

that she wasn't speaking of Simenon at all—that she was referring to someone else entirely. *Nikolas, maybe?* But Nikolas had been dead for months already. Surely, Gerda Idun couldn't have been thinking of *him*.

No, Scott assured himself. She was talking about the loss of Simenon. She *had* to be.

Sitting down beside Gerda Idun, he kept her company in her time of need. He didn't say anything else. He just sat there with her on the edge of the platform.

After what she had been through, it was the least he could do.

As the *Stargazer* made her way around the star called Wayland at full impulse, Picard surveyed the work being done on his bridge.

The equipment damaged in the ship's encounters with the Balduk was undergoing rapid repairs, thanks to a half-dozen of Simenon's best engineers. It seemed they were all over the place, lying on their backs under half-reconstructed consoles or propping up new plasma conduits.

Unfortunately, it would be some time before the rest of the *Stargazer* could be restored to full working order.

The captain hoped that wouldn't be a problem when they arrived at their destination, which would be in just a few minutes. Vigo had made the situation sound fairly desperate.

"Captain," said Paxton from his comm console, "sensors are picking up a vessel in orbit around Wayland Prime."

The one Vigo warned them about, no doubt. "On screen," said Picard.

A moment later, he saw what they were up against. It was a Pandrilite vessel, made more for cargo transport than armed conflict. However, appearances could be deceiving.

"Hail them," he told Paxton.

The com officer bent to his task. A minute later, he looked up and said, "No response, sir."

"Engineers, clear the deck," said the captain.

Simenon's people didn't have to be told twice. They stopped what they were doing and piled into the turbolift.

Picard glanced at Paris, who was still filling in for Vigo. "Are we in weapons range?"

"Not yet, sir."

"Captain," said Paxton, "the Pandrilite is coming out to meet us."

Picard could see the cargo ship looming larger on his screen by the moment.

He was glad that Kastiigan wasn't on the bridge. But then, he had made it clear that he wanted the science officer to stay in his section while they approached Wayland Prime.

"Weapons range," Paris reported.

Picard nodded. "Thank you, Mr. Paris. Target their weapons ports and—"

Before he could get the rest of the order out, his viewscreen filled with a blinding flash of crimson light and the bridge rocked with the impact. Obviously, the Pandrilite meant to fight.

After the beating the *Stargazer* had taken at the hands of the Balduk, she wasn't exactly battle-ready. But Picard would be damned if he was going to run from *this* fight.

"Fire phasers!" he barked.

Twin energy bolts shot out from the *Stargazer*'s phaser batteries and speared their adversary. From where the captain sat, they looked like direct hits.

"Again!" he snapped.

Paris activated the beams a second time and skewered the Pandrilite in the same place.

"We've disabled their phaser banks," Paxton reported.

Picard took some satisfaction in that. "Try hailing them again, Lieutenant."

This time, the com officer had a bit more success, if the Pandrilite visage that showed up on the screen was any indication. The fellow's jaw muscles fluttered with barely suppressed fury.

"What in the name of the Virtues do you think you're doing?" he demanded.

"This is Captain Jean-Luc Picard of the *Stargazer*," Picard said. "To whom do I have the pleasure of speaking?"

"How dare you!" the Pandrilite railed. "We're here to pick up one of our people—a fellow named Ejanix. There's been a tragedy in his family and—"

"Sir," Paxton interjected, "they're preparing to go to warp!"

Here? thought Picard. So deep inside a star system? Did they know how big a chance they were taking?

Obviously, they were desperate to get away. But even if they were willing to risk destroying themselves, the captain wasn't about to give them the opportunity.

"Target their nacelles," he told Paris, "and fire!"

On the smaller monitor embedded in his armrest, Picard watched their phaser beams trace fiery paths across the void—and again hit what they aimed for. Both the Pandrilite ship's nacelles erupted with white-hot fury and went dead.

The Pandrilite captain glowered at him from the larger screen. "I'll see to it you're court-martialed for this!"

"My apologies," Picard said archly, "for my weapons officer's itchy trigger finger. I promise it won't happen again."

The Pandrilite didn't seem to know what to say to that.

"That is," the captain added, "as long as you lower what's left of your shields and cooperate with my boarding parties. Otherwise, I can't promise you we won't blow you out of space altogether."

That didn't seem to sit well with the Pandrilite. However, there wasn't much he could do about it.

"You and I will chat later," Picard promised his adversary. Then he terminated the communication and made arrangements to send out a half-dozen shuttles—five of them to the Pandrilite vessel and one to the planet's surface.

He had a feeling that Vigo would be glad to see it.

Epilogue

GERDA LOOKED DOWN at her raw, red hands, which—like her face—hadn't completely healed yet.

"Another day or so," she said, in answer to her sister's question. "As long as I don't miss any regeneration sessions."

Idun nodded from the other side of the room. "I am glad to hear that."

They were sitting in Gerda's anteroom, and had been for the last several minutes. However, they had yet to bring up the subject they both needed to speak about.

"I understand you piloted the shuttle that went down to the installation," Gerda ventured.

"I did," Idun confirmed. "But there wasn't any fighting. Vigo had already freed the engineers, secured the installation, and rounded up the intruders by the time we arrived."

"No battle, then," Gerda concluded.

"None," said her twin.

They looked at each other.

"I apologized to Refsland," Gerda offered. "I told him I was wrong to have manhandled him—no matter what he might have been thinking about me."

"What did he say?"

"He accepted my apology."

"That was generous of him."

"I thought so as well."

Gerda had apologized to Greyhorse as well—for doubting his love and his loyalty. But she was careful not to mention that.

Again, they regarded each other. Finally, it was Idun who broke the ice—as she had to, under the circumstances.

"I was surprised," she said, "when I heard about Gerda Idun."

Gerda nodded. "Everyone was."

Idun shook her head. "Not you, surely. You knew about her from the beginning."

Gerda shrugged. "I had my suspicions. But I didn't know anything for certain."

Idun frowned. "I should have been suspicious too. Instead, I trusted her. I was so fascinated with the novelty of there being three of us..."

"It's understandable."

"No," said Idun. "It's not. Our father on Qo'noS taught us to be wiser than that."

"Our father also taught us to be generous," Gerda told her sister, "and to open our hearts. And I wasn't prepared to do that. But you were."

Her sister looked pained. "What went on between us...it was stupid."

"Childish," Gerda added.

"I regret it."

"So do I," said the navigator.

Idun's expression turned thoughtful. "She wasn't all that different from us, I think."

"No," said Gerda, "she wasn't. Though she may have opposed us, she was a warrior."

Idun grunted. "A warrior."

And she would need to be, Gerda mused. If what Gerda Idun had told Nikolas was true, she and her people would continue to have a fight on their hands. For Gerda Idun's sake, Gerda hoped they would win.

"Come," said Idun. "It's time for our shift."

Together, they left Gerda's quarters and headed for the turbolift down the hall. As they made their way along the corridor, the navigator was pleased that her hands and face weren't the only things that had begun to heal.

Something even more important to her had begun to heal as well.

Coming in September 2003

STARGAZER

OBLIVION

Chapter One

JEAN-LUC PICARD waited for the brassy octagonal portal in front of him to iris open. Then he stepped through the aperture, leaving what had once been the ribbed and heavily reinforced cargo bay of an Yridian freighter and entering a very short, dimly lit corridor.

In two strides, he reached another octagonal portal at the corridor's far end. As before, he waited for it to open like a flat metal flower. Then he emerged into the sprawling, low-ceilinged armory of a Tellati warship.

Of course, there weren't any weapons in this armory—not anymore. But Picard had seen enough Tellati hulks to recognize the rows of durianium clamps set at intervals in the bulkhead, designed to hold enough disruptor rifles for the needs of a Tellati crew.

Picard doubted that the armory's original owners would have approved of the bright, jazzy music currently wafting through it, or the airy, blue lighting, or the buttery fragrance that teased the captain's nostrils.

But then, the armory was now serving as a bar of sorts—just as the cargo bay Picard had just left behind had been recast as the lobby of a rather seedy-looking spa.

In fact, if he kept walking through enclosure after enclosure and navigated correctly, he would find himself traversing bits and pieces of a great many vessels—not just Yridian and Tellati, but Klingon and Ubarrak and Orion, and on and on—a seemingly endless list of them.

Together they formed a strange and shadowy city—a city in orbit around a world that had never had life of its own. A city called Oblivion.

Or rather, that was the nickname it had been given by the earliest Terrans to frequent the place. In the original Ubarrak, it was called Obl'viaan.

Picard didn't know how or why the first two ships in the by now immense complex had been cobbled together, or even by whom. No one did, apparently—or at least, no one seemed willing to admit it.

But little by little, other ships had been added—derelicts and sections of derelicts, space stations and half-destroyed hulks of space stations, some old and some relatively new, some easily recognizable and some not. And gradually, the city called Oblivion had taken on a purpose.

It had become a place where merchants of all species and backgrounds could gather—where they could peddle their wares and fashion their deals without the specter of interstellar politics looming over them.

It didn't matter who was at war with whom. In Oblivion, traders from both sides of the conflict could still carry out their transactions in peace—regardless of whether they were selling medicines, high-yield explosives, or the latest in exotic entertainments.

Nothing was forbidden in that regard. No commercial activity was off-limits.

But for all its license, Oblivion wasn't a lawless place. Far from it. Like any city, it had its government and its laws, and a security force to see that they were obeyed.

Like the orbital city's merchants and traders, security was made up of many different species. However, those represented in the greatest numbers were either Ubarrak, human, or members of a people who had only recently given the Federation cause for concern...

A people who called themselves Cardassians.

As Picard took in the room, with its several humanoid denizens sitting in front of the bartender or scattered among tables, he remarked yet again to himself how fertile Oblivion would be for scholarly inquiry.

Even from an archaeological perspective—his favorite since his days at the Academy—there was much to study. Where else could one find the aft section of a hundred-year-old Meskaali squadron fighter? Or a Rigelian ore transport of a perhaps even earlier vintage?

Unfortunately, Picard hadn't been able to spend the nearly two days since his arrival merely scratching his archaeological itch. He had been familiarizing himself with this portion of the city, with an eye to carrying out his mission here.

And an unusual mission it was. Quite a change of

pace from his normal duties, which called for him to direct the activities of an entire starship.

In Oblivion, Picard was responsible only for directing his own activities. He wasn't even wearing his Starfleet uniform, having exchanged it before he left for civilian garments.

It was rare for a Starfleet captain to skulk around undercover, much less to do so entirely on his own. However, on this occasion, he had no other option.

When an opportunity of this magnitude came up, one was compelled to seize the day.

In fact, he would be seizing it in less than half an hour. But he didn't want to show up at his rendezvous point too soon, lest he attract undue attention.

Picard could have returned to his hotel, but it was a little too far away for comfort. He preferred to remain there at the bar, which was only a short walk from his destination.

And no one would question the notion of a man sitting in a bar for half an hour. He would fit right in.

Besides, all that walking in the dry, controlled environments of Oblivion had made him rather thirsty.

Aiming to address that problem, the captain crossed the room and took one of the few empty seats in front of the bartender—a human-looking female, though appearances were often deceiving in a place like Oblivion. There were a number of species that looked human but were anything but.

At the moment, the bartender was attending to a Tellarite—a corpulent, white-haired specimen—who was in the midst of what seemed to be a long-winded tale, if the eye rolling of his fellow patrons was any indication.

"And then," the Tellarite said in that blustery tone characteristic of his species, "I told him to take his phase coils and get out of my sight. I'd been trading too long to lay out good credits for shoddy merchandise. 'Shoddy?' he bellowed. 'You wouldn't know a quality phase coil if it was inserted into your left nostril!' Naturally, I wasn't going to stand for that sort of abuse..."

Picard could see why the other patrons were rolling their eyes. Unless one was a dealer in phase coils, the Tellarite's saga was anything but riveting.

Still, the bartender didn't take her eyes off the Tellarite. She hung on his every word, no matter how uninteresting it might have been to anyone else.

And she wasn't just listening because she had to, it seemed to Picard. She was listening because she wanted to, because she *enjoyed* it.

Of course, it might just have been an act to help business. But if it was, it was a bloody good one.

The captain didn't even mind having to wait to place his order. He was content for the moment to watch the woman smile a knowing smile at the Tellarite and fill his mug with something viscous and ocher-colored.

The Tellarite seemed to appreciate it too, if his delighted snorts were an accurate measure. And his species wasn't known for getting along very well with humans.

Picard admired anyone who did a good job, whether it was commanding a starship or maintaining a food replicator. And the bartender wasn't doing just a *good* job—she was doing a *great* one.

It would have been nice to have such a person doling out drinks on the *Stargazer.* There was plenty of stress involved in serving on a starship. A bartender in the right setting would go a long way toward helping everyone unwind.

Unfortunately, it wouldn't have been even remotely practical for the captain to place a bar in the *Stargazer*'s cramped little lounge. And even if he could shoehorn it in somehow, he doubted he could bend regulations enough to staff it with non-Starfleet personnel.

As he pondered the idea, the woman moved down the bar and turned her attention to Picard. "What can I get you?" she asked, smiling at him as warmly as if they were old friends.

Very old friends.

In fact, Picard had to wonder for a moment if they had actually met before. But he ruled out the possibility in short order. He had an impeccable memory when it came to faces, and the bartender's wasn't at all familiar to him.

Nonetheless, he found himself smiling back at her. "Tea," he said. "Earl Grey, if you've got it. Hot."

"Oh," she said, "I've *got* it, all right."

Turning around, she punched a code into the replicator mechanism on the wall behind her. A soft, yellow glow became visible through the device's transparent door. When it subsided, she opened the door and removed a steaming cup.

Even before she placed it in front of the captain, he could smell its soothing aroma. *Earl Grey,* he thought with a rush of contentment.

"There you go," said the bartender. "You know, I don't get many requests for tea, Earl Grey or otherwise."

The captain grunted. "Really."

She tilted her head as if to get a better look at him. "Obviously, you're from Earth."

"I am," he said, "yes."

"But you don't miss it much. You'd much rather be out here, where every moment brings the possibility of adventure."

It was true. Picard could have followed in the footsteps of his father, a distinguished vintner, but instead he chose to make a career for himself among the stars.

But was his thirst for exploration that obvious? So much so that a person he had barely met could sense it?

"Are you sure about that?" he asked.

The woman nodded. "Pretty sure. When you meet as many people as I do, you develop a knack for knowing what makes them tick."

The captain wanted to speak with her further—on that or any other topic, well into the night if he'd had the time. Her manner was that pleasant, that inviting.

But he *didn't* have the time. He was on a mission. And pretty soon, it would call him away.

"Impressive," he told the bartender.

Then Picard made a point of looking around the place, as if he had some real interest in the furnishings. By the time he turned around again, the woman had moved down the bar to one of her other customers.

Obviously, she had taken his hint. He breathed a sigh of relief—until he realized that the patron next to him was staring at him.

She was human, in her late twenties if he was any judge of such things, her long, charcoal gray dress and elaborate hat of the same color concealing what appeared to be an unremarkable height and build.

Still, the captain might have called her attractive if not for the look in her dark brown eyes. It was a desolate look. A look that spoke of loss and missed opportunities, of pain and humiliation...of surrender.

It struck Picard that she was the exact opposite of the woman who was tending bar. This person seemed dead inside, hollowed out by some terrible ordeal, while the bartender couldn't have been more alive.

"Do I know you?" he finally asked the woman.

She stared at Picard a moment longer. Then she said, "You've got hair."

It was a bizarre observation, to say the least. "Apparently so," he responded.

The woman's eyes narrowed. "You don't remember...?"

The captain looked at her. "Remember *what?*"

Her brow puckered as if in disappointment. "No," she said with what sounded strangely like regret. "Of course you don't."

Picard didn't want to leave it at that—not after she had fired up his curiosity. But his mission prevented him from pressing her for the information.

After all, if she *did* know him, she could expose him for who he was—and that would pretty much throw a hyperspanner in the works, wouldn't it? So his best bet was to remain silent and hope it was a simple case of mistaken identity.

The woman stared at him a moment longer, as if she were inclined to say something more to him. Then, with a deep and uncomfortably prolonged sigh, she shook her head and turned back to her drink.

And he turned back to his.

But as Picard sat there sipping his tea, he continued to watch his neighbor out of the corner of his eye—and every so often, she would sneak a peek at him. Apparently, she still couldn't decide if he was who she *thought* he was.

Less than eager to give her a chance to do so, he finished his tea as quickly as he could. Then, plunking down the appropriate coinage as payment and tip, he left the bar and the woman in the hat behind him.

But the incident had thrown off the captain's timetable. He had hoped to nurse his tea for a while, to linger over it. Now he would have to move at an all-too-leisurely pace, perhaps even loiter here and there, or else reach the location of his intended rendezvous too soon.

Picard sighed. In every plan, there was an X factor—an unexpected element. The woman in the elaborate hat had been such an element.

He could only hope there wouldn't be any others.

Look for STAR TREK fiction from Pocket Books

Star Trek®

Star Trek®: The Original Series

Star Trek: The Next Generation®

Novelizations

Far Beyond the Stars • Steve Barnes
What You Leave Behind • Diane Carey

Books set after the series
    Homecoming • Christie Golden

Enterprise®

Novelizations
    Broken Bow • Diane Carey
    Shockwave • Paul Ruditis
    By the Book • Dean Wesley Smith & Kristine Kathryn Rusch
    What Price Honor • Dave Stern
    Surak's Soul • J.M. Dillard

Star Trek®: New Frontier

New Frontier #1-4 Collector's Edition • Peter David
    #1 • *House of Cards*
    #2 • *Into the Void*
    #3 • *The Two-Front War*
    #4 • *End Game*
#5 • *Martyr* • Peter David
#6 • *Fire on High* • Peter David
The Captain's Table #5 • *Once Burned* • Peter David
Double Helix #5 • *Double or Nothing* • Peter David
#7 • *The Quiet Place* • Peter David
#8 • *Dark Allies* • Peter David
#9-11 • *Excalibur* • Peter David
    #9 • *Requiem*
    #10 • *Renaissance*
    #11 • *Restoration*
Gateways #6: *Cold Wars* • Peter David
Gateways #7: *What Lay Beyond:* "Death After Life" • Peter David
#12 • *Being Human* • Peter David

Star Trek®: Stargazer

The Valiant • Michael Jan Friedman
Double Helix #6: *The First Virtue* • Michael Jan Friedman and Christie
    Golden
Gauntlet • Michael Jan Friedman
Progenitor • Michael Jan Friedman

Star Trek®: Starfleet Corps of Engineers (eBooks)

Have Tech, Will Travel (paperback) • various
    #1 • *The Belly of the Beast* • Dean Wesley Smith
    #2 • *Fatal Error* • Keith R.A. DeCandido
    #3 • *Hard Crash* • Christie Golden
    #4 • *Interphase, Book One* • Dayton Ward & Kevin Dilmore

Miracle Workers (paperback) • various

> #5 • *Interphase, Book Two* • Dayton Ward & Kevin Dilmore
>
> #6 • *Cold Fusion* • Keith R.A. DeCandido
>
> #7 • *Invincible, Book One* • Keith R.A. DeCandido & David Mack
>
> #8 • *Invincible, Book Two* • Keith R.A. DeCandido & David Mack

Some Assembly Required (paperback) • various

> #9 • *The Riddled Post* • Aaron Rosenberg
>
> #10 • *Gateways Epilogue: Here There Be Monsters* • Keith R.A. DeCandido
>
> #11 • *Ambush* • Dave Galanter & Greg Brodeur
>
> #12 • *Some Assembly Required* • Scott Ciencin & Dan Jolley

No Surrender (paperback) • various

> #13 • *No Surrender* • Jeff Mariotte
>
> #14 • *Caveat Emptor* • Ian Edginton
>
> #15 • *Past Life* • Robert Greenberger
>
> #16 • *Oaths* • Glenn Hauman

#17 • *Foundations, Book One* • Dayton Ward & Kevin Dilmore

#18 • *Foundations, Book Two* • Dayton Ward & Kevin Dilmore

#19 • *Foundations, Book Three* • Dayton Ward & Kevin Dilmore

#20 • *Enigma Ship* • J. Steven and Christina F. York

#21 • *War Stories, Book One* • Keith R.A. DeCandido

#22 • *War Stories, Book Two* • Keith R.A. DeCandido

#23 • *Wildfire, Book One* • David Mack

#24 • *Wildfire, Book Two* • David Mack

#25 • *Home Fires* • Dayton Ward & Kevin Dilmore

#26 • *Age of Unreason* • Scott Ciencin

#27 • *Balance of Nature* • Heather Jarman

#28 • *Breakdowns* • Keith R.A. DeCandido

#29 • *Aftermath* • Christopher L. Bennett

#30 • *Ishtar Rising, Book One* • Michael A. Martin & Andy Mangels

Star Trek®: Invasion!

#1 • *First Strike* • Diane Carey

#2 • *The Soldiers of Fear* • Dean Wesley Smith & Kristine Kathryn Rusch

#3 • *Time's Enemy* • L.A. Graf

#4 • *The Final Fury* • Dafydd ab Hugh

Invasion! Omnibus • various

Star Trek®: Day of Honor

#1 • *Ancient Blood* • Diane Carey

#2 • *Armageddon Sky* • L.A. Graf

#3 • *Her Klingon Soul* • Michael Jan Friedman

#4 • *Treaty's Law* • Dean Wesley Smith & Kristine Kathryn Rusch

The Television Episode • Michael Jan Friedman

Day of Honor Omnibus • various

Star Trek® Short Story Anthologies

Strange New Worlds, vol. I, II, III, IV, V, and VI • Dean Wesley Smith, ed.
The Lives of Dax • Marco Palmieri, ed.
Enterprise Logs • Carol Greenburg, ed.
The Amazing Stories • various

Other Star Trek® Fiction

Legends of the Ferengi • Ira Steven Behr & Robert Hewitt Wolfe
Adventures in Time and Space • Mary P. Taylor, ed.
Captain Proton: Defender of the Earth • D.W. "Prof" Smith
New Worlds, New Civilizations • Michael Jan Friedman
The Badlands, Books One and *Two* • Susan Wright
The Klingon Hamlet • Wil'yam Shex'pir
Dark Passions, Books One and *Two* • Susan Wright
The Brave and the Bold, Books One and *Two* • Keith R.A. DeCandido

STAR TREK

STARGAZER: OBLIVION

MICHAEL JAN FRIEDMAN

In 1893, a time-traveling Jean-Luc Picard encountered a long-lived alien named Guinan, who was posing as a human to learn Earth's customs.

This is the story of a Guinan very different from the woman we think we know.

A Guinan who yearns for oblivion.

Available September 2003

STAR TREK®
THE STARFLEET
SURVIVAL GUIDE
AVAILABLE NOW... FOR THOSE
WHO PLAN AHEAD.

STSG